Also in the *X Libris* series:

Back in Charge	Mariah Greene
The Discipline of Pearls	Susan Swann
Hotel Aphrodisia	Dorothy Starr
Arousing Anna	Nina Sheridan
Playing the Game	Selina Seymour
The Women's Club	Vanessa Davies
A Slave to His Kiss	Anastasia Dubois
Saturnalia	Zara Devereux
Shopping Around	Mariah Greene
Dares	Roxanne Morgan
Dark Secret	Marina Anderson
Inspiration	Stephanie Ash
Rejuvenating Julia	Nina Sheridan
The Ritual of Pearls	Susan Swann
Midnight Starr	Dorothy Starr
The Pleasure Principle	Emma Allan
Velvet Touch	Zara Devereux
Acting it Out	Vanessa Davies
The Gambler	Tallulah Sharpe
Musical Affairs	Stephanie Ash
Sleeping Partner	Mariah Greene
Eternal Kiss	Anastasia Dubois
Forbidden Desires	Marina Anderson
Pleasuring Pamela	Nina Sheridan
Letting Go	Cathy Hunter
Two Women	Emma Allan
Sisters Under the Skin	Vanessa Davies
Blue Notes	Stephanie Ash
Pleasure Bound	Susan Swann
Educating Eleanor	Nina Sheridan
Silken Bonds	Zara Devereux
Fast Learner	Ginnie Bond

Chrysalis

Natalie Blake

An *X Libris* Book

First published by X Libris in 1997

Copyright © Natalie Blake 1997

The moral right of the author has been asserted.

*All characters in this publication are
fictitious and any resemblance to real
persons, living or dead, is purely coincidental.*

All rights reserved.
No part of this publication may be reproduced,
stored in a retrieval system, or transmitted, in
any form or by any means, without the prior
permission in writing of the publisher, nor be
otherwise circulated in any form of binding or
cover other than that in which it is published and
without a similar condition including this condition
being imposed on the subsequent purchaser

A CIP catalogue record for this book
is available from the British Library.

ISBN 0 7515 1958 8

Photoset in North Wales by
Derek Doyle & Associates, Mold, Flintshire
Printed and bound in Great Britain by
Clays Ltd, St Ives plc

X Libris
A Division of
Little, Brown and Company (UK)
Brettenham House
Lancaster Place
London WC2E 7EN

Chrysalis

Chapter One

'*YOU'RE NOT GOING* to hide yourself in your room for tonight's party, are you, Pippa?' Alexandra said, cornering her flatmate as she skirted round the streamers and balloons which seemed to have taken over the living-room of their small flat.

'Well, I—'

'Pip! You *can't* duck out of this one! It's supposed to be to celebrate the end of the run.'

'Or drown our sorrows,' Pippa said drily.

Alexandra rolled her eyes. 'Honestly, what an optimist you are!'

Pippa shrugged. 'Sorry. I can't see that being out of work is cause for celebration, that's all.'

'And that's why you don't want to come to the party?' Alex eyed her cynically and Pippa knew that she could see right through her.

'You know I'm not really a party animal,' she defended herself weakly.

Alex shook her head, exasperated. 'I don't know why you chose this business, I really don't. I've never met a more unsociable performer. What is it, Pip, is that wonderful persona you put across on stage really a total act? Or is it just that you don't like mixing with the guys?' Eyeing Pippa shrewdly, she noted the way her pale skin reddened betrayingly. 'That's it, isn't it? You know, in the six months we've known each other I've never known you go out on a date.'

Pippa felt the old, familiar panic churning through her veins and knew she had to deflect Alex before she probed too deeply.

'You sound like my mother!' she said in a feeble attempt at lightness. 'Look, I'll show my face at the party, all right? Anything for a quiet life!' She rolled her eyes comically and threw up her hands as she headed for her room, making Alex laugh.

Inside the sanctuary of her bedroom, Pippa plonked herself down on the dressing-table stool and stared at her reflection in the age-speckled mirror. The dark blue eyes gazing back at her looked too big for the small, pale oval of her face. There was still a trace of a blush on her cheeks and, not for the first time, Pippa cursed her delicate Celtic skin for betraying her.

Didn't Alex see? In a way, she had hit the nail on the head, as it were, when she pointed out that Pippa was completely different on stage. As an actress she could slip into the skin of someone else, assume a fictional character to whom she had no responsibilities once she left her behind. A person no one expected anything from.

Slowly Pippa unravelled the braid she had plaited in her long, red hair. Running her fingers through it, she pulled the weight of it off her shoulders so that she looked like Monica Heller, her character in the play that had just come to an end.

'You want me, lover?' she murmured in Monica's sultry, low-toned voice. 'Come and get me!'

Pippa chuckled softly to herself, pleased that she could transform the inexorably bad lines into something sexy and convincing. Picking up her hairbrush, she sighed, wishing that she could inject her own pathetic little life with even a modicum of the excitement of the characters she portrayed in the theatre.

'Liar,' she murmured to herself, 'you know you'd run a mile if anyone noticed you.'

That was the crux of the matter – interesting people drew others to them, exposed themselves relentlessly to scrutiny. Pippa couldn't stand that, preferring instead to take a behind-the-scenes role in real life, leaving centre-stage for the theatre.

'You live in a fantasy world – you ought to be put away.' The hard, sneering voice forced its way out of the locked chamber of her memory, making her hide her face in her hands and shake her head from side to side. How could a memory have the power to hurt her so much after all this time?

But it did. Though she tried to shut it off, she could still feel the imprint of rough, cruel hands crawling over her body, could still smell the nauseous mixture of beer fumes and stale, masculine sweat as she struggled and squirmed.

I don't want this! The thought came back to her, like a scream. She had screamed the words then, before they were drowned by her sobs of shame and shock and pain. Then they had been met by drunken laughter, and a second pair of hands had moved to hold her down . . .

'No!'

Pippa's head jerked up and she stared furiously at herself in the mirror. She would not let her one and only failed attempt at intimacy haunt her like this. It should never have happened, *she* should never have *let* it happen!

With the self-blame came anger, washing over her like a tidal wave. Pippa welcomed it, preferring anger to terror. Anger helped her to see that the incident had, in some warped, unwelcome way, done her a favour. At least now she knew what could happen if she allowed her roles to spill over into real life. She knew what men were capable of – and she knew to keep out of their way.

Tying her hair into a loose ponytail, she pushed the hateful memories roughly aside and went to help Alex prepare for the party.

Matt Jordan lay back on the king-sized hotel bed and surveyed the pretty blonde standing uncertainly at the end of it. She didn't look nearly as sure of herself now that they were alone together as she had when she had pursued the studio car halfway across London in the hope of catching a glimpse of him. There had been no sign of hesitation when she'd whispered obscenities in his ear while he signed his autograph on the delicate, peach-furred flesh of her forearm.

'How old are you?' he asked, alarmed suddenly by her reticence.

What was her name? Lisa . . . Laura . . . *Lauren*, yes he remembered now – *to Lauren, with undying love, from Matt Jordan*. Her choice of words, not his.

'Lauren?'

She smiled as he said her name, as if she had been having second thoughts about coming into the hotel with him, but was reassured by the fact that he remembered her name. Perhaps she thought that made her less of a tramp, Matt thought sourly. If he knew her name before he screwed her, maybe that was what she called a 'relationship'.

'Old enough,' she said, her body language changing, opening out.

Her voice was certainly mature, he recognised, watching as her fingers toyed with the button at the vee of her blouse.

'Undress for me,' he coaxed.

The girl smiled seductively at him as she complied, slipping the buttons smoothly through the buttonholes of her blouse, as if she'd practised in front of a mirror. Matt watched her, his eyes masking his thoughts. What would she think if she knew he always asked them to strip first so that he could reassure himself that there were no hidden cameras, no tape recorders supplied by the tabloids to set him up? He'd already made sure that she left her shoulder bag in the living-room of the suite and closed the bedroom door firmly behind them.

Christ, when did it all get this sordid? he wondered as he watched her. When did suspicion – paranoia, some called it – and boredom set in? He considered, briefly, sending her away, but she looked so fresh and young and *ripe* . . . Matt leaned forward, smiling at her as she leaned forward and released her firm full breasts from the lacy cups of her bra.

Matt swung his legs over the side of the bed, his interest quickening.

'Nice,' he murmured in the voice he knew they all loved. 'Come here.'

He peeled off the shorts himself. They were bleached denim cut-offs which nestled in the tender crease between her legs and buttocks, leaving little to the imagination. As he hooked his thumbs into the waistband of her wispy panties, he caught the heavy, musky scent of her sex and felt his cock begin to stir.

He wouldn't send her away, he decided, not yet. The night was young, the girl was willing and he was lonely, so bloody lonely. With a ragged sigh, he pressed his face against the fragrant, inverted triangle at the apex of her thighs and breathed in deeply.

'Oh – Matt!' the girl whispered, transported, it seemed, by the small gesture.

Ignoring her, Matt rubbed his cheek against the soft, downy skin of her stomach, drawing her closer so that she was standing between his outspread legs.

He liked the fact that he was still fully clothed while she was naked. It made him feel more in control, *safer*. He frowned, wondering at the curious thought. Since when had he felt *out* of control in any part of his life, never mind on occasions such as this? Since when had he wanted sex to be *safe*?

Impatient with himself, he drew the girl down so that she was kneeling on the carpet between his legs. His breath caught in his throat as he saw the way she was looking at him: adoring, pliable – *trusting*. He felt the unwelcome weight of responsibility descend as he cupped her face in his hands and gazed into her clear blue eyes.

'Are you sure you want to do this?' he asked.

She looked surprised for an instant, then she smiled, a small, knowing smile that made his pulse race. It told him forcefully that this was no innocent girl, carried away by a crush on a film star. *Was that what he'd wanted to believe she was?*

Matt closed his eyes for a moment. Where the hell had that mocking voice in his head come from? Deliberately closing it off, he opened his eyes and returned the girl's smile. Slowly he lowered his head and caught her lips between his. They tasted sweet, like ripe cherries, and he dragged the tip of his tongue delicately along the inner surface.

'You taste good,' he murmured against her mouth.

'So do you,' she replied, snaking her arms up around his neck and pressing herself against him.

Matt could feel the contours of her body moulding against the hard planes of his chest. Suddenly he didn't want to be clothed any more, he wanted to feel the warm silk of her skin against his.

She sat back on her heels and watched him as he unbuttoned his shirt and threw it aside before pulling off his shoes and socks. The fastener to his trousers caught briefly and he yanked it open, standing up to ease his trousers and underpants down his long thighs. Naked now, he sat back down again, eyeing the girl quizzically.

Noticing that he wasn't fully erect, she reached for him, expertly wrapping her fingers around the quiescent stem of his penis. Matt swallowed as he felt the tension gathering in his scrotum and his cock reared up, angry red against the pale skin of her small hand.

She smiled, a small, triumphant smile that she had been able to arouse him so quickly. Glancing at him through her lashes, she licked her lips before drawing the tip of his glans between them.

The sensation of her soft lips sucking so gently on the end of his penis was exquisite. Matt could feel the slow burn of desire begin to unfurl through his veins, chasing away any doubt that still lingered. God, he needed this!

Slowly she drew him further into the hot, wet cavern of her mouth, until her lips were fastened over the sensitive rim of his glans. Matt leaned forward and cupped the back of her head. He could feel the tender curve of her skull beneath his fingers, the paradox of fragility and strength of her skin and bone.

She was doing strange, wonderful things with her tongue. It flickered randomly over the velvet-soft skin of his glans, tantalising and teasing him until he felt a tear of fluid leak out into her mouth.

It was as if she had been waiting for this as a sign, for she cupped his balls and squeezed gently, moving his testicles in their sac of loose skin, making it tauten and swell. With her other hand, she stroked the now bone-hard stem of his penis, sending shivers of pleasure along its length, making his breath catch.

She was good, he acknowledged silently.

'Enough!' he said, forcing himself to withdraw.

Lauren lifted her head and looked at him through overbright, lambent eyes.

'Don't you like it?' she asked plaintively.

The question reminded him once again of her youth and he hid a smile.

'Too much,' he admitted, pulling her up into his arms. 'I don't want it to be over too soon.'

She looked puzzled.

'I'm not in any hurry,' she said.

This time, Matt did smile.

'Then let's take our time,' he said, gathering up one firm breast and feeding it into his mouth.

He could feel the beat of her heart against his lips as he left her nipple and moved across to the curve of her bosom.

She moaned softly as his lips trailed from one breast to the other, brushing lightly over the tips of her nipples before dipping down to lick the delicate, slightly salty skin in the fold below her breasts.

Her fingers tangled themselves into his hair, pulling slightly as he bored the very tip of his tongue into the deep crevice of her navel.

'Ooh! Yes!' she whispered as he blew softly on the narrow expanse of flesh which separated her navel from the blonde curls of her pubic hair.

Holding her by the narrow cage of her hips, Matt brushed his lips against the light smattering of fair hair. It was soft, the skin underneath warm and pink. His tongue probed the tip of the crease that hid her innermost flesh. He felt her shudder before she slowly moved her feet apart.

Her sex unfurled, exposing the perfect, shiny pinkness of her inner labia. Matt felt his pulse quicked as he saw that the small promontory of her clitoris had slipped from its protective hood. He imagined it quivered in anticipation. Slowly he leaned forward and placed a tiny kiss on its tip.

Lauren gasped and she clutched convulsively at the side of his head. Glancing up at her, Matt saw that her eyes were closed, her expression one of total absorption. He smiled, confident now that there was no ulterior motive to her being here. Relaxing, he brought his thumbs to the edges of her crease and gently pulled apart her labia.

Using his tongue, he traced the intricate folds of flesh, pressing the tip into the dewy channels either side of her inner labia before turning his attention to the weeping fount of her womanhood. Her secretions were like warm honey on his lips. As he probed the entrance to her vagina, he felt her muscles contract around his tongue, trying to draw him in. Deliberately tantalising her, he withdrew, allowing his tongue to brush lightly up to her clitoris.

The little bead was pulsing gently now, waiting for him to draw it between his lips. In this, Matt did not disappoint her. Sucking gently on the hard little nub, he allowed his teeth to graze the tip before stabbing the very end of his tongue against it.

Lauren went wild. He felt her clitoris spasm against his lips and he pressed the flat of his tongue against it, hard, absorbing the shockwaves. Her legs seemed to buckle and Matt caught her round the waist, supporting her as she was overcome.

Judging the precise moment when her climax peaked, he pulled her onto his lap so that her legs were resting on his and the tip of his penis found the entrance to her body.

'Oh yes!' she shouted, squirming on his lap so that he penetrated her with one swift, sure thrust.

Matt closed his eyes for a moment and forced her to be still. He didn't want all sensation to be lost in a frantic race towards his own orgasm. Instead he wanted to relish the sensation of her hot, silky tube enclosing him, wanted to feel the last vibrations of her climax around his cock.

She was panting, her skin gilded with a fine film of perspiration. A light, flowery perfume seemed to be oozing from her pores and Matt buried his face in the narrow cup of her shoulder. He felt surrounded by her; by her scent, by her soft skin and by the convulsing flesh of her sex.

Slowly at first, he began to move. Lauren moaned softly as he rocked his hips. The penetration was deep, but due to their position Matt's range of movement was limited. Lauren gripped his hips with her knees, twining her arms around his neck so that she wouldn't fall backwards.

Matt rubbed his face against the soft flesh of her breasts, absorbing the erratic thud of her heartbeat. His own was pumping hard, the adrenalin rushing through his veins as he felt the familiar gathering in his scrotum.

He shivered as something seemed to give in the base of his cock, like a valve opening to let the semen surge through. Pressing his hands against the small of her back, he held her still as the ejaculate pumped out of him, flooding her sex and making her body jerk against his.

It was some moments before they finally peeled apart.

'Wow,' Lauren said, brushing her hair away from her face with her hands, 'that was something else!'

Matt watched her as she climbed off his lap and went to gather up her clothes. She dressed quickly as if, now that the deed was done, she couldn't wait to get out of the hotel room.

'You said earlier that you weren't in a hurry,' he said, reaching for his trousers.

'Well—'

'I could buy you dinner, if you like.'

He made the offer diffidently, wondering why

he felt the need to prolong the encounter. As if by getting to know her a little he would be able to imbue it with some meaning.

'Sorry, I can't.' She leaned forward to kiss him on the lips. 'It was great though. Wait until I tell my mates that I screwed Matt Jordan! They are going to die!'

She was laughing, so young and carefree. Matt smiled back, hiding the melancholy which was spreading through him. They said goodbye and she went, presumably to regale her friends with stories of his prowess. Matt wondered why he felt used, when he had taken what he wanted from her in the same way she had from him.

Wearily, he dragged himself into the bathroom and splashed his face with cold water. In the mirror over the sink, he stared at his reflection and wondered when his eyes had grown to look so dead, so bleak.

As the party grew louder, their guests relaxing under the influence of alcohol and, judging from the sickly sweet smells oozing into the atmosphere, other, less legal substances, Pippa felt herself becoming invisible. Her face ached from the constant social smiling, her head ached with the effort of being congenial without giving too much of herself away.

She watched now, comfortable in her accustomed role as an observer, glad to be freed from the obligation of small talk. There was Alex, tongue to tongue with the male lead, Jonathon Devereaux.

Pippa suppressed a shudder, wondering how her friend could bear it, let alone enjoy such an activity. Jonathon was a nice enough guy, if a bit dim, but the thought of making love with him . . .

'You all right, Pip?'

She jumped as Simon Standish, her husband in the play, appeared at her shoulder. Close behind him was a young man, barely out of his teens, dressed from neck to foot in matt black leather.

'You haven't met Darren, have you?' Simon said now, introducing her. 'You two chat while I go and open another bottle of plonk, okay?' He moved off through the crush of people, leaving them alone.

'Hello.' Pippa smiled at the young man, able to relax knowing he was no threat if he was with Simon.

'Hi.' Darren spoke in a false falsetto that set Pippa's teeth on edge.

'Are you an actor too?' she asked, at a loss as to what to say in the ensuing silence.

'Ooh no,' Darren said, tapping her playfully on the shoulder as if she had cracked a particularly funny joke. 'I'm strictly rental.'

'Oh.' Pippa didn't know what to say. It was all very well being party to the gossip that Simon was partial to paying for his pleasures (no commitment, darling), it was quite another thing to be faced with the reality.

She appraised Darren coolly, wondering what motivated him to sell himself for sex. Without being judgemental, she was fascinated. Maybe she could use the knowledge in a future role. Just as she was about to bombard him with questions, Simon reappeared, opened wine bottle in one hand.

'Looks like I've saved you from a fate worse than death, Darren,' he said cheerfully as he refilled the mugs they had had to use once Alex and Pippa's meagre supply of glasses had been exhausted.

'What do you mean?' Darren glanced sidelong at Pippa, his nervousness suddenly palpable. 'You're not a cop, are you?'

Simon threw back his head and roared with laughter.

'Pippa is an *ac*-tor', aren't you, darling?' he said, slinging a casual arm around Pippa's shoulders. 'A very good one, too. From the look on her face she was about to start dissecting you – weren't you, Pip?'

Making a face, Pippa slid out from under his arm, finding its weight oppressive.

'Something like that,' she admitted.

'Darling, I can read you like a book!'

Pippa smiled faintly and sidled away. God, she was tired. Gradually the crush of people began to thin as excess took its toll, or the promise of a new venue to continue the revelry beckoned. Once begun, the exodus gained momentum. Pippa gladly took on the task of finding coats and ushering their guests to the door. The hallway filled to the sounds of goodbye kisses and shrill farewells until, at last, she found herself alone.

Glancing round the wreckage of their living-room, Pippa decided to leave the clearing up until morning. Alex had disappeared and Pippa was glad that the inevitable dissection of the evening could be put off for now. With a sense of relief, she headed for her room. Opening the door, she felt for the light switch.

'Je-sus – put the bloody light out!'

Pippa leapt back out of the room as she saw that her bed was occupied by a couple she had never seen before. The man was naked, his skinny white buttocks poised above the partially clad body of a woman whose face Pippa couldn't see.

'Oh! Sorry,' she mumbled, thoroughly embarrassed. She was about to back out of the room and leave them to it when her outrage asserted itself. This was *her* room, for goodness sake! 'Actually, this is my room and I'd appreciate it if you'd leave. Now,' she said boldly.

The man looked at her in astonishment.

'*Now?*' he echoed disbelievingly.

'Yes.' Pippa stood her ground, holding the door wide.

Glancing down at his wilting penis, the man shrugged.

'The damage is done now, anyway – c'mon, Sam – let's move.'

The girl sat up, grumbling. Pippa saw that she was drunk and confused and she turned her head away so that she didn't have to watch them dress.

'Party pooper,' the man said mildly as he passed her, flashing her a grin. His girlfriend was more belligerent.

'You fuckin' frigid, or what?' she snarled, pushing her face close to Pippa's.

The man rescued her.

'Leave it, Sam. Sorry.' He made an apologetic face at Pippa as he dragged the girl away.

Pippa saw them out, shutting the door firmly behind them and locking it before going back to her room. *Frigid*. The word was so stark, so uncompromising, but that, she guessed, was probably the word to describe her. It meant sexually cold, didn't it? Well, she was certainly that.

Going over to the bed, she stripped off the sheets and threw them in disgust into the corner of the room. She opened the window to allow the cool, fresh night air to blow away the frowsy scent of cheap perfume and sex while she changed into her pyjamas.

When, at last, she climbed into bed, she closed her eyes and pulled the quilt protectively up to her chin. The covers enfolded her, making her bed feel like sanctuary. *What's the matter with me?* she thought, feeling tears of self-pity gathering in the corners of her eyes. *No one else seems to have a problem with sex.*

She could hear the sounds of Alexandra's bedsprings straining through the thin wall between their bedrooms. Gradually the tempo quickened and Pippa could hear her friend's low moans growing more frantic, rising to a crescendo.

I can't bear it! The words bounced around in Pippa's head and she burrowed under the pillows, trying to block out the noise. Alex was screaming now, as if she was in pain, and Pippa clenched her teeth. She could hear the low rumble of Jonathon's voice as he joined Alex at the peak. Then there was a period of gasping and sighing that somehow seemed worse than the screams.

Pippa felt hot and restless. Tossing and turning, she pushed back the covers and rubbed at her arms through the thin cotton of her pyjamas. Her breasts pressed together and she was at once conscious of the delicate scrape of the material against her nipples.

Lying on her side, she drew up her knees, stroking the downward slope of her breasts gently, as if for comfort. She hated the way Alex flaunted her sexuality so openly in front of her, even while she knew that her friend had no idea of the effect it had. Listening to her making love night after night made Pippa feel so uncomfortable, stirring feelings and longings that she would prefer to leave undisturbed.

Slowly she eased her hand into her pyjama bottoms and slipped the middle finger into the warm furrow of her sex. As she had known it would be, the tender flesh was slick with moisture.

Closing her eyes, Pippa touched herself gently, stroking the sensitive nub of her clitoris so that little waves of pleasure began to ripple outward from that small spot, filling her with warmth. Her mouth and throat felt dry and she shifted restlessly, yearning for she knew not what.

You fuckin' frigid, or what? The girl's slurred, mocking voice came back to her, acting like a bucket of cold water over her senses. Squeezing her thighs tightly together, Pippa trapped her hand between them, helpless to stop the tide of her feelings from ebbing away.

It was always the same – she simply wasn't a sexual being and she might just as well accept the fact. Some people were made that way, she told herself reasonably, and she was one of them. It was pointless to torture herself by striving for more.

Pulling the covers up around her chin, Pippa forced her muscles to relax, making herself breathe deeply and evenly. It was a long time before she slept.

Chapter Two

'*YOU DON'T WANT* to work on the next Tarantino, you won't talk to the whisky people about a commercial – what is this, Matt, are you thinking of retiring, or what?'

Matt regarded his friend and agent from his vantage point by the window and smiled at his agitation. Brad was beginning to look his age; his dark hair was streaked with silver and his genial features had settled into contented lines, like a comfortable quilt. When frowning, as he was now, two deep lines were scored between his eyes which stayed for several minutes after his expression lightened.

'Relax, Brad – your ten per cent is safe,' Matt drawled.

'So – what *do* you want to do?' Brad spread his arms wide and shrugged expressively.

Gazing out of the window across the dreary, rain-washed London rooftops, Matt sighed as he contemplated his reply.

'I guess I'm feeling a bit stale, y'know?' Glancing

across at his friend he saw that Brad didn't know what he was talking about. His words confirmed it.

'If you had a mortgage as big as mine and three kids to feed, clothe and educate, you wouldn't have the luxury of "feeling stale". Fucking bachelors, I hate the lot of you,' he grumbled without rancour.

Matt laughed.

'How *are* Moira and the kids?' he asked.

'Demanding,' Brad replied at once, then his face softened and the twinkle came into his eye that was always there whenever he spoke of his family. 'Charlotte starts school in September and Rebecca will take her place at kindergarten. Georgie's nearly walking now—'

'Walking? He couldn't even crawl when I saw him last!'

'Yeah, well that just goes to show how long it is since you came over! Moira's always on at me to drag you over for dinner when you're in town.'

'Give her my love and tell her that I might even make it this time. I can't believe my god-daughter's old enough to start school already. You're a lucky guy, Brad, having Moira and a family like yours.'

'Right – like, lucky bankrupt, you mean?' he said, resorting to bluff to hide the depth of his feelings. Brad hadn't missed the wistful note in Matt's voice, though, and he knew that, for all his old friend's fame and fortune, he wouldn't swap places with him for a day. 'Any news in the settling-down department yourself, Matt?' he asked slyly, knowing that Moira would quiz him later.

Matt thought of his encounter with the starstruck fan the night before and grimaced.

'Tell Moira she'll have to keep her wedding hat in storage for a while yet,' he said flippantly. 'Now come on, Brad – you must have something for me that'll spark a bit of interest?'

Brad sighed. 'How about reading for the romantic lead in this musical?' he suggested, half in jest. Matt hadn't been on stage since his film career took off ten years before. Brad raised his eyebrows as Matt picked up the script, but he held his tongue as he flicked through it.

'Maybe that's what I need; the buzz of a live audience,' Matt murmured, half to himself.

'The money's crap,' Brad warned.

'So's life, but who's complaining?' Matt said, pushing the script into his briefcase. 'I'll give you a call when I've read this,' he said.

'Come to dinner,' Brad said firmly. 'Moira and the kids would love to see you.'

Matt's expression took on the wistful cast Brad had noticed earlier.

'Yes,' he said, as if suddenly making up his mind, 'yes, I will. I'd love to see them too. Call me, Brad.'

'I will.'

The two men shook hands and Matt left the office feeling far happier than he had when he'd entered it.

Pippa and Alex couldn't believe their luck when, barely a month after their play closed, both were sent scripts for a new musical.

'Wouldn't it be great if we got to work together again?' Alex enthused as she read the script of *Chrysalis* at the breakfast table.

'Yes.' Pippa knew that their convenient arrangement of sharing the flat would become difficult if one of them was working and the other wasn't, and she was secretly relieved that the situation hadn't arisen to date. She liked Alex, despite her apparently inexhaustible sex drive, and she wouldn't be able to afford anywhere nearly as comfortable as this without her. Unlike Pippa, Alex was heavily subbed by an indulgent father, so unemployment would not have been such a hardship for her – at least, not financially.

'What part are you up for?' Alex asked now, through a mouthful of Rice Krispies.

'Molly Brown,' Pippa replied absently, her attention caught by the script.

As she read, she realised with a dart of excitement that it was really rather good. Her agent, whom she shared with Alex, had been enthusiastic on the phone. She seemed to think that Molly Brown would be a good springboard for Pippa, a worthy successor to her last role.

'Molly Brown? That's quite a big part, isn't it? I wonder why I'm not being put forward for that too?'

Alex's tone was petulant and Pippa suppressed an inward sigh. 'What has Dolores suggested you for?'

'The chorus. Again.'

'Oh.'

Pippa didn't know what to say. The truth was that, though Alex was a competent singer and dancer, she lacked that certain something that would make her stand out on stage. As Dolores, their agent, had confided to Pippa in a rare moment of indiscretion, 'Honey, Alexandra is all *oomph* and no substance.'

'Bloody typical – Dolores always puts you up for the good parts and leaves the dross for me! It's not fair.'

'Thanks, Alex,' Pippa said drily.

'I didn't that mean you aren't good enough,' Alex said hastily. 'It's just . . . well, you know.'

Pippa picked her words carefully. 'Cheer up, Alex – I wouldn't call the chorus of a top West End musical "dross".'

'D'you think it could be big, then?'

Pippa shrugged. 'I heard a rumour that they're going to offer the part of Antony to Matt Jordan.'

'*Matt Jordan?* Phew, that *would* be a crowd puller! Can he sing?'

'I suppose he must be able to.' Pippa frowned, wondering if the rumours were true and, if they were, whether Matt Jordan would accept the role. This kind of show needed name-power to succeed. If the show was a success, it could be that the role of Molly Brown would be the break for which Pippa had worked so hard.

I want this role, she thought fiercely. Picturing her mother and father in the small, Hertfordshire village where she had grown up, Pippa smiled inwardly. How wonderful it would be to be able to send them tickets to *Chrysalis*! They had attended every single show in which she had ever appeared at least once, no matter how small her role. If they saw her as Molly Brown, Pippa knew they would be thrilled.

'Oh well,' Alex said now, breaking into Pippa's daydreams, 'we've got a few days before the auditions so we might as well prepare.'

Pippa nodded absently. She was going to do more than prepare, she promised herself. By the time she arrived at the auditions she would *be* Molly Brown.

The Connaught Theatre was a huge, imposing Victorian edifice close to Piccadilly circus. Pippa felt the adrenalin begin to pump through her veins as soon as she stepped through the stage door into the gloomy rabbit warren of corridors and stairs which led to the dressing-rooms.

The chorus had been auditioned the day before and Alexandra had come home full of optimism for her own chances. Apparently, the rumour was correct – Matt Jordan was to take the leading role, with Diana George as his leading lady. All that remained now was for the supporting actors to be cast.

There were several 'Molly Browns' in a dressing-room backstage. Recognising one or two faces, Pippa nodded and smiled, but did not allow herself to be drawn into the general buzz of nervous chatter. Positioning herself in the corner, she gathered herself, determined to remain calm and unruffled.

Molly Brown was to sing two solo numbers in the show, each quite different. As her rivals for the part were called one by one, Pippa listened as they invariably chose to belt out the brash, bluesy song in preference to the ballad. Most were very good. Pippa hoped she hadn't misjudged by spending more time practising the ballad until she felt she had the pitch and tone just right. Supposing the director only asked for the other number? She could sing it, of course, but Pippa had no doubt that she could give her best account of herself with the slower song.

They must have directed each aspirant out through another door, for no one returned to the small dressing-room. Finally, when there was only Pippa and a small, dark-haired girl left, Pippa's name was called.

'Break a leg!' her companion said.

Pippa swallowed hard, telling herself that the moment she stepped onto the stage her nerves would have steadied. She hoped she was right because she'd never be able to sing if she continued to feel this nauseous!

It was impossible to see into the auditorium once Pippa was on stage, but at least she felt better. Taking centre stage, she gazed out into the darkened theatre. She had prepared a short scene which she delivered as best she could, trying not to think of the unseen eyes watching her so critically.

As soon as she began to sing she forgot about her nerves, embracing the melody and allowing herself to be carried away by the haunting, poignant ballad. Her voice soared as she hit every note squarely, her voice pure and strong, reverberating through her slight frame. As she finished, she heard voices muttering in the auditorium. For a moment, she felt disorientated, taking a few seconds to come back down to earth and remember where she was.

A man rose and walked into the light. Tall and balding, wire-rimmed spectacles perched on the end of his nose, he consulted his clipboard.

'Thank you, Miss ... ah ... Brooks. Yes.' He looked up and beamed at her. 'Could you give us "Summer's Day", please?'

'Of course.'

Pippa forced herself not to consider the fact that she hadn't heard any of the others sing both numbers. Though she barely allowed herself to hope, she let her mounting excitement through sufficiently to put a bounce in her step as she moved in time to the music.

'You are my summer's day ...' Once again, Pippa sang her heart out. When the last bars faded, she looked expectantly at the director. He was scribbling on his clipboard with a pencil.

'Thank you, Miss Brooks,' he said without looking at her. 'We'll be in touch. Next!'

Pippa felt as if someone had just thrown a bucket of ice-cold water over her. Had she messed up the second song? As she was ushered away by an assistant, she felt a cloud of melancholy descend.

'Miss Brooks?'

She turned to see a man slipping through the door which led to the auditorium. He was tall and dark-haired with the kind of face so beloved of billboard posters – square-jawed with strong, symmetrical features. As he stepped out of the shadows, she saw that the eyes appraising her were a clear, sparkling blue, the pupils large and well-defined.

'Mr Jordan,' she said, recognising him at once.

He smiled at her, a wide, mega-watt smile that, had she been susceptible to such things, Pippa was sure would have bowled her over completely. Recognising that the curious sinking feeling in her stomach was a natural reaction to meeting such a big star so unexpectedly, she returned his smile politely.

'I didn't realise you were in the theatre.'

'I like to take an interest,' he said. 'I'm glad I was here today – you have a very beautiful voice.'

'Thank you, Mr Jordan – it's a pity the director doesn't share your enthusiasm!' She made a face and Matt Jordan laughed.

'Don't be so sure he doesn't,' he said enigmatically.

Pippa stared at him, conscious of a sudden, irrational racing of her heart. Matt Jordan's eyes had darkened, his gaze moving slowly over her face, lingering on her lips. She caught her breath as he unexpectedly reached out and touched the corner of her mouth with his fingertips. Desire, white hot and uncompromising, seared through her, making her recoil.

'I – I have to go,' she stuttered, fighting the familiar, nauseous panic that rose up in her chest. Turning on her heel, she virtually ran away from him and out into the street.

What on earth had *that* been about? she wondered as she emerged from the gloom into the bright light of the day. Maybe her disappointment at the director's response had been too clear, prompting him to console her, one performer to another.

She smiled cynically. Why would a major Hollywood star give two hoots about a struggling actress like herself? It was probably all part of the audition – catching her off-guard so that he could judge the natural cadences of her voice.

That didn't explain why she had had such a peculiar reaction to him. Yes, there had been the panicky fear she always felt whenever a man touched her, but she knew there was more to it than that. The churning in her stomach had been due to something else, something quite alien to her.

Taking her place in the bus queue, Pippa tried to turn her thoughts away from the uncomfortable notion that she had probably made a total ass of herself. Hugging her script to her chest, she prayed that Matt Jordan had influence and that maybe, just maybe, she would be called back.

Matt waited until the last audition was over before approaching Lee Broadbent, the director.

'Well?' he said.

Lee turned and looked quizzically at him.

'Well, what, Matt?' he asked.

'You'll be casting Pippa Brooks as Molly Brown?'

'With respect, Matt, *I'm* the director – it is my decision,' Lee said stiffly, avoiding Matt's eye.

'Of course. I'm not trying to step on your toes, Lee. I just thought that she was far and away the best we've seen.'

'Yes. Very attractive too.' Lee looked at Matt coldly. 'You'll know my decision in due course.'

Matt watched as the man strode away. So that was how it was going to be, was it? You jumped-up Hollywood star, me director – know your place. *Christ*, Matt thought, *I hope I haven't messed up the girl's chances*. He wouldn't put it past Lee Broadbent to refuse to cast Pippa Brooks purely to show Matt who was in charge.

That would be one hell of a pity. Surely he hadn't been the only one who saw how she lit up the stage when she performed? Lee's snide innuendo about her looks was a cheap shot. Sure, the girl was attractive, but Matt had his pick of beautiful women. He wasn't generally easily swayed by a pretty face.

There was something about Pippa Brooks, though . . . for a moment after she had stepped into the spotlight, Matt had thought that he knew her. He had to admit to himself now that it was that sense of recognition that had sparked his interest. And the way she had fled when he touched her . . . what had made him do that anyhow?

'Matt – darling!'

He was distracted by the arrival of Diana George, his leading lady. Descending on him in a haze of *Poison* and cigarette smoke, she wrapped her arms around him and crushed him against the hard humps of her silcone implants.

'How *are* you? I was *so* thrilled, darling, when I heard you were to play Antony to my Angela! Let me look at you.' She stood back and ran her eyes over him critically. Before Matt could say anything at all, she was off again. 'Still gorgeous, I see! Darling, we're going have *such* fun. Just like Monaco. Do you remember Monaco?'

Matt smiled insincerely. In Monaco he had worked with Diana one stiflingly hot summer and made the mistake of starting an affair with her. Diana's subsequent demands had almost ruined the film and he had been trying to forget the experience ever since.

'Of course,' he said, deftly removing himself from her clutches, 'how could I ever forget? Are you here to watch the auditions?'

Diana made a dismissive gesture with her fingertips.

'I was passing, merely,' she said, speaking, as she always did, as if she were reciting lines learnt for a play. Dropping her spent cigarette carelessly on the floor, she ground it out with her heel and relit another. 'I must be going, darling – *so* much to do. See you when rehearsals start.'

She strode out of the auditorium, leaving Matt

feeling breathless. He'd forgotten what a pain Diana George could be.

'When you luvvies have *quite* finished,' Lee said acidly.

Seeing that they were about to start auditioning for the part of Daniel Brown, Molly Brown's husband, Matt sat down with a sigh. This venture hadn't started well.

'It's not bloody fair!' Alex stormed as soon as Jonathon arrived for the evening. 'Pippa got the part of Molly Brown in *Chrysalis* and I got a part in the bloody chorus!'

'Hey – that's a reason to celebrate! Well done, Alex—'

'Aren't you listening to me, you moron? Pippa got Molly Brown.'

'It should have been you, baby,' Jonathon told her dutifully.

'Of course it should have been me! If I'd been given the chance to test for the part, it *would* have been me. It's out and out sodding favouritism, that's what it is.'

The adrenalin was coursing through her veins, making her jumpy. Pacing the living-room floor, she eyed Jonathon with unwarranted belligerence. He had thrown himself on the sofa and was watching her with a wary look in his eye. Alex felt a different kind of agitation trickle through her veins as she turned on him.

'Why are you looking at me like that?' she snapped.

Jonathon's eyes widened, the pupils dilating so that there was barely a rim of dark brown iris left around the perimeter.

'I was just thinking how beautiful you look, baby.' His voice was throaty, signalling that he was in the mood to play.

Alex ran her eyes over his thick, chestnut brown hair, down to the cultivated petulance of his face. A boy's face on a man's shoulders, a man's body...

'Did I tell you you could look at me?' Alex said coldly.

Jonathon's adam's apple bobbed as he swallowed convulsively.

'No,' he whispered.

'So why are you looking?'

Hands on hips, Alex leaned forward from the waist, looming over him and giving him a tantalising glimpse of the shadowed cleft of her cleavage. She was wearing a low cut, scoop-necked top over a long skirt, with ankle boots. Everything was black, from the thick kohl around her eyes to her nail varnish. Jonathon's eyes flickered over her as he ran his tongue over his lips.

'I can't help it,' he whispered. 'You look fantastic today.'

Straightening, Alex flounced over to the mirror which hung above the fireplace and gazed at her reflection. Her straight brown hair was piled up on top of her head, exposing the slenderness of her neck. She had been heavy-handed with her make-up, outlining her eyes with black kohl and painting her full lips a bruised, matt plum colour. Her green eyes burned as if with fever as she stared at herself, and she felt the beginnings of a slow-burning arousal flicker into life in the pit of her stomach.

Turning back towards Jonathon, she smiled slowly at him.

'Take off your clothes,' she purred.

His eyes darted nervously towards the door.

'In here? But Pippa—'

'Pippa will be out all day. She's gone to visit her parents in the sticks. Now – are you going to strip, or am I going to have to do it for you?'

Jonathon stood up slowly, holding her gaze. Alex loved the glazed expression in his eyes. The sense of power she felt over him always thrilled her, turning her on in a way that straight sex never did.

'Am I going to have to whip you, Jonathon?' she asked him conversationally. 'Is that what you want? Is that why you're taking your time – to antagonise me?'

'No, Alex,' he said, his fingers fumbling with the buttons of his shirt.

Though his denial was emphatic, both of them knew that he was lying. And both of them knew that, how ever hard he tried to please her, she would whip him anyway if that was what she decided to do.

There was a slight sheen to his skin as he shrugged off his shirt and began to unbuckle his belt. The sharp, salty tang of male arousal hung in the air and Alex felt her nipples harden, her breasts swelling and pressing against the flimsy fabric of her blouse as she watched him. His hands trembled slightly as he unfastened his trousers and pushed them down to his ankles.

Alex smiled cruelly, her eyes lighting on the hard shaft of flesh which bobbed hopefully between his thighs as he straightened.

'Well, well, we are excited, aren't we?' she mocked, enjoying the expression of abject misery which passed across his eyes. It was this combination of humiliation and excitement, of reluctance and eagerness that gave her such an intense thrill.

'Alex—'

'Shut up!' Suddenly she felt incredibly irritated. 'If you can't keep quiet, then get out right now!' she snapped.

Jonathon's eyes opened wide, brightening with panic as he realised that she was serious. Holding her eye, he bent down slowly to pull his trousers and underpants free.

'Leave them,' Alex said, relishing the flush this curt command brought to his cheeks.

Jonathon's eyes flickered nervously towards the door again and Alex realised that he didn't quite trust her assertion that Pippa was not due back any moment. Smiling inwardly, she allowed her eyes to pass slowly over him, not bothering to temper her expression of haughty disdain.

'What a pathetic article you are, Jonathon. If only your fans could see you now; your trousers round your ankles and your cock fit to burst. What was it that critic said about you? Something about your "darkly erotic stage presence ... Jonathon Devereaux is *all* man".'

Jonathon winced visibly and Alex laughed.

'Maybe I should take a photo and send it to her? She wouldn't have the hots for you for long then, my darling, would she?'

With every insult, Jonathon's penis twitched in convulsive ecstasy. Alex felt her own sex-flesh swell and moisten at this obvious sign of her power over him. Though it was true, he did look ridiculous with his trousers round his ankles, somehow that did not detract from his essential masculinity. He had the kind of body that only a true narcissist could have sculpted.

Running her eyes over his finely honed muscles, Alex admired the smooth sheen of his skin. Last time he came, she had spent a self-indulgent hour massaging baby oil into his skin. She enjoyed the feel of his firm flesh beneath the pads of her fingertips, liked to pinch and scratch at his skin so that the surface turned pink and she could capture his shuddering sighs in her mouth ...

She wouldn't touch him like that now. Tonight she wanted to prolong the delicious feeling of power, of control, for as long as possible.

'Wait,' she said, striding from the room and making for her bedroom.

At the back of her wardrobe she kept a large cardboard box which she liked to call her box of tricks. Inside she kept a selection of whips, canes and sex toys. Choosing a large, pink-skinned dildo, Alex shoved the box to the back of the wardrobe and marched into the living-room again.

Jonathon hadn't moved, though his eyes followed her nervously as she walked past him. Alex saw the flash of disappointment cross his eyes when he realised she hadn't brought in a whip.

'Not for you, darling,' she purred as his eyes fell on the obscenely large vibrator.

Alex twisted round a chair so that she could sit and face him.

'Now,' she crooned softly, relishing the growing apprehension in his eyes, 'I want to watch you make yourself come.'

'Alex – no!' Jonathon was clearly appalled at the suggestion, and Alex realised that she had never played this particular game with him before. So much the better – she always liked it more when the tension was running high. She loved to taste the uncertainty, verging on fear, that her lovers inevitably showed towards the unknown.

Holding Jonathon's eye, she ran the tip of her tongue around her lips, moistening them as, at the same time, she allowed her eyelids to droop and her head to fall back slightly on her shoulders, exposing the slender white column of her throat.

Jonathon's hand hovered at his groin as he watched her, his fingers curling around the firm shaft of his penis as Alex ran her fingertips lightly down her neck to her breasts. She felt her nipples harden beneath the flimsy fabric of her blouse, thrusting forward as if begging for attention.

'That's right,' she whispered, leaning forward to

watch him, 'stroke it slowly . . . '

She watched as Jonathon, apparently oblivious now to the fact that he was still standing in the middle of the living room with his trousers down, began to masturbate in earnest. As she watched his hand move up and down the length of his swollen shaft, she lifted the hem of her skirt and folded it back several times.

Underneath she was wearing black panties with a thong back and a tiny triangle of lace at the front which had worked its way securely into the cleft of her sex. Jonathon stared at her exposed pussy with unconcealed excitement, his fist moving faster at his groin.

Alex stroked the vibrator along the delicate rim of her sex-lips before positioning the head directly above the tip of her clitoris. With the fingers of her other hand, she stroked the soft, puffy folds of flesh on either side of the thong, marvelling at how wet she was already.

Jonathon was clearly close to climax. He looked hot and distracted as he moved his hand back and forth and even from across the room, Alex could see that he was trembling. Slowly, with great deliberation, she twisted the base of the vibrator so that it began to buzz softly.

'Aah!' she breathed raggedly, closing her eyes as the gentle vibrations travelled through her body.

Suddenly it was as if Jonathon did not exist. Having aroused her he had discharged the role she wanted him to play, leaving Alex free to seek her own satisfaction.

Twisting the base, she increased the intensity of the vibrations so that shards of heat sliced through her belly and upper thighs, turning her stomach to water and her legs to nerveless jelly.

It was coming. Radiating out from the tiny point at the apex of her labia which was the focus of her every sexual response, the sensations came quicker, more sharply as she raced towards the inevitable climax.

Suddenly, shockingly, an image of Matt Jordan's picture-perfect features pushed itself to the forefront of her mind. Alex imagined that it was his tongue and not the cold, inflexible plastic which pressed against her clitoris and flicked against the convulsing flesh surrounding it. Yes – he would make a pretty sight, his dark head crushed between her thighs.

Matt Jordan was the key to improving her role in *Chrysalis*. If she could manoeuvre him into kneeling between her legs like this, then all her problems would be over. All men were biddable if you gave them what they wanted. The trick was working out what really turned them on.

Alexandra smiled as she came. The part of Molly Brown was all but hers – she normally got what she wanted. And she wanted Matt Jordan. The idea crystallised in her mind as her orgasm flowed through her, giving her renewed energy and rendering the man now shooting his seed all over her fake-fur rug all but redundant.

Switching off the vibrator, Alex smoothed down her skirt and stood up.

'Clean that up before you leave,' she said indifferently to Jonathon before striding straight past him without so much as a backward glance.

'But Alex . . . ' Jonathon gazed after her miserably, sensing that it was over.

Chapter Three

IT WAS ODD how a look, a gesture, should take on such importance in her mind. Pippa tossed and turned in bed, unable to get the disturbing incident with Matt Jordan out of her head. After the audition she had successfully put the memory aside. Now, with the news that she had got the part she wanted, it came back to haunt her.

As clearly as if it were happening before her again, she saw him emerge from the auditorium into the corridor. Even at the memory, she felt her stomach lurch as it had then. Her memory wavered as she tried to recall exactly what he had said to her. All she could remember was the way he had looked at her, and the gentleness of his fingertips as he reached out to touch her.

'Oh God!'

Throwing back the covers, Pippa paced to the window and gazed out into the darkness. It was a clear, starry night and the muted night-noises of the city seemed to be a long way below. Recognising her reaction to Matt Jordan as desire did not make it any easier to face. She could do without the distraction.

Turning her back on the benign night sky, Pippa threw herself onto the bed. He had known how she felt, she was sure of it. Now that she had got the part, would he expect her to act on the desire which had flared between them?

If only I could. Pippa rolled onto her back and stared up at the darkened ceiling. It had been a while since she had truly regretted her lack of sexual skill. Usually it was sufficient simply to ignore the occasional signals her body sent her and to keep all the men with whom she came into contact at arm's length. Now, though, her skin prickled with awareness, a slow, liquid warmth spreading slowly through her veins as she thought of Matt Jordan.

She'd seen his films, of course, and lusted after him in a detached, vague kind of way. He was an attractive man – well built, though lean, his physique healthy-looking rather than pumped-up. The roles he played were usually action-packed with a strong romantic element. Whatever part he played, Matt Jordan always got the girl, even if he didn't always want to ride off into the sunset with her.

Seeing him on the silver screen was one thing, but to come face to face with the object of one's secret lust, a prime player in one's fantasies, was a powerful experience. She hadn't expected him to be as attractive in the flesh as he was on screen.

In the enclosed space of the corridor, his famous

presence had been overwhelming, too much. Maybe that was what had made her feel dizzy, so uncharacteristically vulnerable? The familiar fear had been there when he touched her, but it had been overlaid by something else, something undeniably pleasant and far more powerful, and for the first time Pippa felt a glimmer of hope.

Closing her eyes, she trailed her fingers up her bare arms to the sensitive hollows of her neck. His touch had been so gentle, and yet so sure. Sweeping her fingertips lightly down to her breasts, she circled one before stroking the palm of her hand across the softly rounded shape of her belly. Imagining it was his hand edging closer to the soft red-gold fleece of her pubis, Pippa held her breath, determined to maximise the warm, languorous feeling which was so unfamiliar to her.

Trailing her fingertips lightly along the cleft of her sex, she felt the warm moisture there and sighed. If only he would touch her like this, so softly, so patiently . . . The petals of her sex opened in response to her restrained caress, her belly tightening with tension as she circled the small protuberance of her clitoris.

It had been so long since she had felt like this, so very long, and Pippa was afraid to breathe lest the feeling should evaporate. Her thighs quivered as the sensations built at the base of her belly. She rubbed lightly at the smooth button at the apex of her labia, gasping at the little sparks of sensation, like electricity, which ran through her, radiating out from the tiny core.

In her mind's eye, she watched as Matt Jordan bent his head, his warm breath brushing against the slippery folds of flesh between her legs. She imagined him leaning forward and placing the smallest of kisses on the very tip of her clitoris . . .

'Oh-h!'

Her climax rippled through her in a long, satisfying wave, filling her with warmth and a curious sensation of weightlessness. Pressing her palm against her vulva to prolong the sensation, Pippa rolled onto her side and curled into the foetal position.

If only her fantasy could extend into everyday life. She would like to be free to explore and caress a lover's body in the same way as she had imagined Matt Jordan caressing hers. She could use her fingers, her lips and tongue to bring pleasure. Yet she was painfully aware that in reality no man would be content with such gentle loving for long. Sooner or later all men wanted to take, to impose themselves in a way that filled Pippa with dread.

Fantasies were best kept within the confines of her own head. Dream lovers could not hurt her, fantasy men could not let her down. Now that she'd got the part of Molly Brown she would have to stay well away from Matt Jordan. It wouldn't do to let him see how attracted she was towards him, not when she was incapable of delivering the kind of loving he would no doubt demand.

That decided, Pippa slipped into an uneasy slumber, fragmented by odd, frightening dreams, interspersed by the most incredible sensations of pleasure. By the time morning came it was apparent that her blithe assertion that she would ignore her attraction towards Matt Jordan was not going to be nearly as easy as she had supposed.

The idea filled her with a cold dread, tempered, she recognised, by a curling excitement which centred itself in her belly.

When Matt went to dinner at Brad's house, he was greeted by a surge of children, all dancing excitedly around his feet. Moira appeared at once to shoo them upstairs and he felt, for a moment, as if he had strayed into a foreign land, a place of chaotic happiness where he had no role. Then Brad pressed a drink into his hand and Moira reappeared looking prettily flushed as she hugged him and he felt enveloped in the warmth of the place, a welcome visitor. He began to relax.

'You're looking very lovely, Moira,' he said, knowing that the compliment would make her blush.

She did not disappoint him, her pale skin growing pink as she laughed.

'You don't change, Matt,' she said lightly.

Though the remark had been an affectionate one, Matt was aware of a blanket of depression settling over him. He had the feeling that Moira had inadvertently hit on what was wrong with him – he was stagnating, standing still while everyone else had moved on.

When the children all reappeared, pyjama'd and groomed by the girl Moira employed to help her, he watched Brad with them with something very close to envy. Maybe it was merely down to getting older, he mused as he sipped his drink. Surely everyone questioned who they were and where they were going at some point in their lives?

Sensing Moira's eyes on him, he turned and smiled at her. Why hadn't he married her when he had the chance, instead of letting Brad steal her from under his nose?

'Penny for them?' Moira said quietly, coming over to perch on the arm of his chair.

He answered in a voice low enough for Brad not to hear above the children's din, 'We were happy together, you and me – weren't we?'

Moira looked surprised. It had always been something of an unspoken agreement between them that they would never speak of what they had meant to each other in the past. Then she smiled and patted the back of his hand.

'For a little while,' she agreed, putting the remark in its proper place. Then she seemed to catch his mood and she was serious again. 'It would never have worked, Matt – we wanted different things.'

Matt nodded, sorry now that he had embarrassed her.

'Yes. I guess I was just checking my memory was working straight. You got what you wanted, Moira, didn't you?' he said as Rebecca rushed up and squeezed her chubby little body between her mother and the visitor, making them both laugh.

As she lifted the child up onto her lap, Moira

fixed Matt with a steady gaze.

'So did you, Matt,' she reminded him. Then she moved away and Matt realised he had never felt this lonely in his life. It wasn't a pleasant revelation.

On the morning of the first day of rehearsals, Pippa felt so nervous she skipped breakfast and went out for a run instead. As she had told her parents, Molly Brown was the most challenging role she had won to date. Once her part was confirmed, she had been sent the whole script to study.

Her character was a 'tart-with-a-heart', a sexy, sluttish girl whose role in the musical, though comparatively small, was pivotal to the plot. Without being conceited, she knew she was up to the role for which she had been picked. If only she could keep her licentious feelings towards Matt Jordan under control!

Alex had no such worries. When Pippa arrived, glowing with exertion, back at the flat, Alex greeted her with a glass of fresh juice and an exuberance which made Pippa feel weary.

'C'mon, Pip – we're supposed to be at the theatre in an hour and you need to shower and change.'

'It won't take me long,' Pippa protested, downing the juice gratefully.

'You're cool about it all, I must say!'

'Am I?' Pippa grimaced, eyeing her friend wryly.

Alexandra was wearing a bright orangy-red

track-suit over a peach-coloured T-shirt. On her feet she wore terracotta-orange jazz shoes which matched the scarf she had tied around her head. There was nothing like making an impression, and Pippa guessed that this was what Alex intended to do. Her friend looked like some exotic bird of paradise.

'You're looking good,' she told her.

To her surprise, Alex flushed slightly.

'Thanks. I'm on the prowl again.'

'Really? What happened to Jonathon?'

Alex shrugged. 'Past his sell-by date, darling.'

'Oh. That reminds me – Jonathon returned the living-room rug. He said he'd had it cleaned . . .?'

Pippa couldn't understand why Alex suddenly couldn't quite meet her eye.

'Oh – he spilt wine on it last time he came . . . hadn't you better hurry?'

Glancing at the wall clock in the kitchen, Pippa nodded and went for her shower.

The Connaught was buzzing with activity by the time Pippa and Alex arrived. Pippa felt the adrenalin begin to pump through her as she absorbed the atmosphere. This was what she loved – the excitement and camaderie of the theatre. The bustle and activity, so purposeful, yet so chaotic as everyone worked towards the goal of production. Somehow each found where they were supposed to be.

'See you later,' Alex said cheerily as she went to join the dance rehearsal which was about to start on stage.

Pippa nodded absently and made her way to the room set aside for her run-through. To her surprise, Matt Jordan stood to greet her as she walked through the door.

'Hello, Pippa,' he said, moving forward to take her by the hand and lead her into the room. 'Everyone – this is "Molly Brown".'

Pippa smiled at the room in general, aware that Diana George was glaring at her. It was awe-inspiring to be resented by so big a star, and Pippa wished fervently that Matt would let go of her hand. She gave a small, experimental tug, but he merely held her more tightly as he introduced the rest of the cast to her one by one.

The chairs in the room had been arranged in a circle, so Pippa was not aware of who was behind her until Matt drew her round.

'And this is "Daniel Brown",' he said, 'Molly Brown's husband.'

Pippa felt as if the floor shifted beneath her feet as she was confronted by the mocking grey eyes of Steve Grainger.

'Steve!' she whispered through lips which suddenly felt stiff and cold.

'You know each other?' Matt asked, seeing her reaction.

Steve smiled the sardonic, lop-sided smile which had haunted Pippa's dreams for so long.

'Pip and I are *old* friends,' he said, drawing out the 'old' so that no one was left in any doubt about how intimate their relationship had been.

'Aren't we, Pip?'

Whereas before Pippa had been embarrassed by Matt Jordan's fulsome greeting, now she was glad to be able to feel the solid warmth of his palm pressing against hers. The bitter taste of bile rose up in her mouth and she swallowed it back, determined not to allow it to beat her.

I don't want this! Staring into Steve's pale eyes, she knew that he remembered as clearly as she did, but that his memory was far different from her own. He had warned her against crying rape, and she never had, knowing it would be her word against his and that circumstances would count against her. She had never heard the term 'date-rape' then. Instead, she had tried to bury the memory so deeply that it could only emerge in her nightmares and in occasional, unpredictable daytime flashbacks that never failed to unsettle her.

How could her luck be so bad that he had been cast in the same musical as her? Steve was a comedian, a television personality with his own series. It was bad enough seeing his hateful, leering face on the screen, but this was worse, much, much worse. It was like confronting a nightmare.

'Are you all right?'

Pippa started as Matt's voice sounded close to her ear and she recognised the note of concern. At once she became aware that everyone was looking at her curiously. Glancing back at Steve, she saw he was enjoying her discomfiture. He, of course, having arrived before her, would have been prepared to see her again, face to face.

Realising how much he was enjoying her humiliation, Pippa made a gargantuan effort to pull herself together. Suddenly it was incredibly important to her to keep the extent to which he had spoilt her life from him. It was bad enough that he was here, that she was going to have to work alongside him – she wouldn't give him the satisfaction of knowing how much seeing him like this had shaken her.

'I'm fine,' she said, amazed and proud of how steadily she spoke.

Smiling tightly at Matt Jordan, she pulled her hand out of his and took the only available seat – which happened to be right next to Steve. Horribly conscious of him as she sat down, she wondered if he had engineered her having no choice but to sit next to him. It would be just the kind of cruel, cat-and-mouse kind of mind-game he had always liked to play with her.

As the focus of attention switched away from her and the read-through began, Pippa realised that not once had it crossed her mind to back out of the play when she saw Steve. It gave her a modicum of satisfaction to know that, though he might have destroyed her confidence in herself as a woman, he hadn't managed to break her.

She shuddered as she suddenly felt his warm breath against her neck as he leaned towards her.

'I'm looking forward to finding out if you've learned a few new tricks since the last time,' he whispered so that only she could hear.

Pippa froze, fighting the nausea which threatened to overwhelm her. Determined not to let him get to her, she gritted her teeth and concentrated on breathing in through her nose and out through her mouth, slowly and evenly.

Sensing that she was being watched, she looked up and caught Matt Jordan's glance. His eyes were filled with puzzled concern. They flickered shrewdly from her to Steve and back again, then he smiled, very slightly, at her. To her surprise, Pippa found herself beginning to relax a little, warmed by his smile, and grateful for the small gesture of support.

Though she was wary of him, she sensed none of the cruelty which was so much a part of Steve in Matt's character. The realisation left her feeling strangely reassured.

Alexandra was not finding her first rehearsal easy. The choreographer was a martinet who insisted on perfection with every step, and pretty soon she felt as though her feet and her calves were on fire.

'Jesus – I thought he'd never stop!' the girl next to her gasped as a break was announced. She had a strong Yorkshire accent which was accentuated by the sexy rasp in her voice which made her sound as if she smoked forty a day.

'His type never do,' Alex replied cynically. 'It's a power game, designed to show us who's in charge.'

'Doesn't he wish!' the other girl muttered.

Alex regarded her with more interest. There was something about the way she spoke, a kind of self-assurance in her tone, that pricked Alexandra's curiosity. Perhaps sensing her scrutiny, she turned bright brown eyes on Alex and introduced herself.

'I'm Francesca – Frankie to my friends.'

They chatted desultorily through the break and Alex spent the rest of the rehearsal covertly watching her new friend. Frankie was a strong, graceful dancer. She had a muscular build that, though slender, was essentially womanly, and her olive-toned skin glowed with good health. In baggy practice shorts, her long, lean legs seemed to go on forever, and the tight cropped top she wore moulded the small but well-defined shape of her breasts.

As they danced, both women grew progressively hotter and sweatier. Being of a similar height, Frankie was moved so that she was dancing beside Alex, and Alex found herself becoming increasingly aware of the other woman's body. She admired the play of her muscles under the taut covering of her skin as she moved. Imagining the springiness of her flesh beneath her fingertips, Alex felt her concentration slipping.

She was good, much better than Alex could ever hope to be, and it came as no surprise when Frankie was moved yet again, this time to dance almost directly in front of Alex. Any jealousy she might have felt towards the other girl was negated by the pleasure Alex derived from watching her dance. She found herself fantasising about running her hands down the graceful sweep of Frankie's back and slipping her fingers inside the waistband of the shorts. Her bare buttocks would feel firm beneath her fingers and she would press her fingertips into the warm, pliant flesh, parting her bottom cheeks and—

'Miss Abbott!'

Alex jumped as the choreographer shouted in her ear. She had been completely oblivious to his approach and was totally baffled as to why he had singled her out. All the women on the stage turned to look at her expectantly and Alex had to bite down on her lip to stop herself from laughing.

Mike Jerome, the choreographer, placed his palms in the small of his back and stretched. Once he had straightened again, he fixed Alex with a gimlet eye and went on the attack.

'You might not be aware, Miss Abbott, but we are here to work. Not to spend our time *ogling* our fellow artistes. *Comprende?*'

Everyone fell about laughing, including, Alexandra was relieved to see, the object of her desire. Frankie winked at her as they all took their places and prepared to re-start the routine. Afterwards, she sought Alex out.

'Would you like to come back to my place for dinner? I was only planning to rustle up a plate of pasta, nothing special, like, but . . .?'

Alex felt desire kick in the centre of her belly, so hard that she couldn't trust herself to speak. She nodded, catching her breath as Frankie reached out and cupped her cheek in a brief, intimate gesture that fuelled her lust by its very simplicity. Towelling herself down quickly, she gathered her things together and was ready to leave in no time.

Frankie lived in a small, pokey flat in a

respectably shabby mansion block, a short Tube ride away from the theatre. They had talked like old friends on the train, discovering that they might well have worked, briefly, in the same production a few months before, though neither remembered the other, and naming mutual friends.

'Here it is – it's not much, but it's home!' Frankie said as she unlocked her front door.

Alex looked around the small, square living-room. It was sparsely furnished with a spindle-legged sofa and a single armchair arranged around a colourful rag rug in front of a three-bar electric fire. The fireplace was lined by dull copper-coloured panels and topped by a mantelpiece of beige tiles. A television set perched precariously on a small, square-topped coffee table in the corner of the room.

Though what little furniture there was in the room clearly came with the flat, everything was spotlessly clean and tidy. Unlike in Alex and Pippa's flat, there were no magazines lying about, or underwear drying over radiators. There weren't even any books or tapes in evidence.

'It's a bit bare, in't it?' Frankie said, picking up on Alexandra's thoughts. 'I only moved in on Wednesday. It'll be okay once I've brought down a few bits and bobs. There wasn't room for much in the car.'

'I'm sure it'll be lovely.' Alex turned to her and smiled.

'Aye, I think so. Would you like to take a shower

before tea? It's through there.'

'Thanks – I was hoping you might say that!'

'Well, old Jerome is quite a taskmaster! I'll have to have one meself before I start cooking.'

Their eyes met and Alex felt again that savage mule's kick of desire in the pit of her stomach. Holding Frankie's gaze, she allowed her feelings to show, and was rewarded by an answering glow in the other girl's eyes. Her pupils dilated and the atmosphere in the room thickened, the sexual tension stretching between them, drawing them closer like an invisible thread.

'Maybe we could save water?' Alex murmured as Frankie came to stand within inches of her.

'Shower together, you mean?' Frankie's voice had dropped an octave, emerging as a husky whisper which rasped over Alexandra's heightened senses.

'It would make sense,' she murmured.

'Oh aye, it would that.'

They were standing toe to toe, so close that Alex could see the yellow flecks in Frankie's brown eyes, could smell the sweetness of her breath and feel the warmth emanating from her body. Alex felt every nerve-ending quiver with tension as she waited for Frankie to bridge the small gap that separated them. She longed to feel the womanly curves pressing against her own, but instinctively held back, waiting for the other woman to take the final step.

Frankie did not reach for her at once as she had hoped she would. Instead, she merely moved her head so that her face swam out of focus and her lips brushed Alexandra's, so gently it felt as if a feather had been drawn lightly across the surface. Alex was unable to suppress a groan of frustration as she stepped back. Frankie chuckled softly.

'Come on,' she coaxed, entwining her fingers with Alexandra's.

The bathroom was cold and bare; the shower cubicle was tiled in plain white; the floor was laid with cracked blue linoleum. Alex barely noticed. Without taking her eyes from hers, Frankie removed the sweatshirt she had pulled on over her dancegear and dropped it onto the floor. Her breasts sprang free from their Lycra-bound restraint as the cropped top followed suit.

Alex feasted her eyes on the firm, rounded orbs. Frankie's nipples were small and brown, the areolae very flat and smooth while the nipples were hard and prominent, like shiny brown acorns. The muscles in her stomach rippled as she bent from the waist to pull down her baggy shorts.

As Alex had hoped, she wasn't wearing anything but a thong underneath which quickly joined her shorts on the floor. She had a thin line of short, black hair on her pubis, but it was so sparse that the tender folds of flesh between her thighs were clearly visible. Alex could see moisture glistening on the lighter, smoother skin of her labia as she moved to turn on the shower.

As the warm spray spluttered through the wide shower head, Alex undressed quickly and joined Frankie in the cramped cubicle. She sighed as the water rolled across her shoulders and cascaded down her back and between her breasts, welcoming the cleansing deluge.

Turning to face Frankie, Alex's breasts brushed against the other girl's hard nipples and her stomach cramped with need. Grasping the initiative, she increased the pressure between them until her own nipples hardened and began to ache. Holding Frankie by the shoulders, she rubbed their wet breasts back and forth, as if trying to ease the ache.

'Here,' Frankie murmured, moving back slightly, 'let me.'

Picking up a bottle of shower gel, she lathered some between her hands and covered Alexandra's breasts. Alex moaned as the most exquisite sensations ran through her. Picking up the shower gel, she followed suit, rolling Frankie's nipples between her fingers and thumbs, then pressing her palms against them, rubbing gently at the burgeoning flesh until Frankie too moaned with pleasure.

As if choreographed, the two women pressed closer together until they were standing, breast to breast, belly to belly, hip to hip. Oblivious now to the water flowing over them, they kissed, tasting each other, sucking and nibbling at their lips and tongues, fuelling the desire mounting between them.

Alex gasped as she felt Frankie's slippery fingers probe the delicate flesh between her legs.

'Oh yes – touch me there . . . frig me, darling . . .'

Frankie murmured endearments into her ear as

she circled her clitoris, sensing exactly how much pressure was required to take Alex to the edge without tipping her over.

'I want to feel your cunt against mine,' she whispered, the words soft, yet shocking.

Alex moaned in protest as Frankie took her hand away and turned off the shower.

'Ssh – come on.'

Dripping from the shower, Alex found herself being pulled into a darkened bedroom.

'Lie down, baby,' Frankie coaxed, leading her over to the bed. 'Spread your legs for me, I want to look at you.'

Alex was so close to coming, she knew she would do anything if it speeded her race to reach the peak. Though she had made love with other women before, she had never been opened and looked at in the way that Frankie was looking at her now. It embarrassed her at the same time as it aroused her, and she wriggled slightly on the soft cotton of the duvet.

'So pretty,' Frankie said softly, ignoring Alex's deflective gesture. 'Later, I want to lick it all over. I want to burrow inside you with my tongue and drink the warm honey that's seeping out of you.'

'Oh God – yes! Please do it, Frankie,' Alex heard herself saying, thoroughly seduced by Frankie's softly voiced obscenities.

'Later, baby. Right now I want to feel your cunt next to mine. I want to grind my clit against yours so that we can both come together.'

As she spoke, she lifted Alex's thigh so that she rolled onto her side. Easing her own legs, scissorwise between Alexandra's, she edged forward on the bed so that Alex's upper thigh was resting against the tautness of her stomach. Leaning forward with a suppleness that only a dancer could hope to achieve, she placed a trail of tiny, openmouthed kisses along Alex's outer thigh. The small, wet kisses sent shivers of delight up and down Alexandra's leg which reached into her lower abdomen with tiny fingers of electrifying pleasure.

She could feel the heat of Frankie's sex inches away from her own, and she longed to feel the slippery flesh meld with hers.

'Please, Frankie,' she pleaded softly.

Frankie chuckled.

'So impatient,' she crooned.

Sliding her bottom along the soft skin of Alexandra's inner thigh, she took most of her weight on her elbows as their labia met in a moist, open-mouthed kiss. Twisting slightly so that her clitoris came into contact with Alexandra's, she moved her hips so that she was grinding against her.

Alex had never experienced anything like it. She could feel the hard little bead of Frankie's clitoris moving back and forth across the tip of hers, could feel the other woman's secretions seeping onto her own moisture-slicked labia. Their swollen, wet sex-flesh made lewd little sucking noises which drove Alexandra wild. After a few moments, she could barely tell where her sex ended and Frankie's began, it was as if they had merged into one moist, pulsating sex.

Suddenly, Frankie stopped grinding and went rigid.

Throwing back her head, she thrust her vulva hard against Alexandra's.

'Push it out, baby – push it out for me!' she urged.

Alex bore down, realising with a thrill that she could feel the other girl's clitoris pulsating as she climaxed. Within seconds, she joined her, crying out with the sheer power of it as she joined Frankie at the peak.

After a few minutes, Frankie peeled away from her and slid up the bed. Taking Alex into her arms, she kissed her lingeringly on the lips. Pulling apart, they smiled at each other contentedly.

'Are you hungry?' Frankie asked, her lips travelling across the smooth skin of Alexandra's forehead. The tip of her tongue tickled across her eyebrows, making Alex shiver. Pressing her own lips against the sensitive area just below Frankie's ear, she answered, 'Mmm. And thirsty. Shall we get up and eat – or stay here?'

Frankie drew her earlobe between her lips and bit gently on it.

'We'll stay here for a bit, shall we?'

Alex sighed and closed her eyes as the other girl nibbled on her ear. She had left the house this morning looking for an affair to replace the one she had had with Jonathon and found it in a most unexpected quarter. Already she could feel the tendrils of re-arousal curling through her body as Frankie moved in close.

Matt Jordan was still her ultimate aim, but she hadn't even come into contact with him yet. Besides, seducing Matt Jordan would only be a means to an end. He could keep. Making love with Frankie was purely for pleasure and, Alex reflected as the other girl kissed a trail down the front of her body, what pleasure!

Chapter Four

PIPPA WAS GRATEFUL for the solitude of the empty flat when Alex did not come straight home from the theatre that evening. She was still reeling from the shock of finding Steve in the rehearsal room. The run-through had gone by in a blur and she had no idea how well, or otherwise, she had performed. Somehow, she had got through the day and found her way home, though she had little recollection of having done so.

However, once she was safe behind the door of her flat, auto-pilot failed her and Pippa slumped onto the sofa, feeling like a wet rag. All day she had been conscious of Steve's physical presence. He still wore the aftershave she remembered and she fancied she could detect the scent of his skin beneath it, sickly sweet and stale. The memories it had evoked had almost made her retch.

Alex was aware that to everyone else in the room, Steve Grainger was in real life as witty, urbane and charming as he was on the TV. No one else would have noticed the often snide remarks made at her expense, the subtle innuendoes which made her feel dizzy with fear.

After that initial reassurance that Matt Jordan had shown her, Pippa had felt very much alone at the rehearsal. It would have been challenging enough to hold her own in a roomful of actors who were all more experienced and, hence, more self-confident than she was, without having to contend with an unwelcome ghost from the past.

Any hopes she might have had that professionalism would overcome Steve's personal vendetta towards her had been dashed by that initial remark. Though the fact that Steve should bear a grudge against *her* seemed to Pippa to be beyond belief.

Wearily she dragged herself into the bathroom and ran a hot bath. Perhaps his ego had taken a knock when she had objected to his violent assault. Certainly he had blamed her at the time for 'inflaming' him, as well as declaring she was deficient as a 'real' woman. He made it sound as though other women actually enjoyed such brutality, that she was somehow odd for objecting.

'Oh God, I don't want to think about it!' she said aloud.

Her voice bounced off the emulsioned walls of the bathroom and echoed in her mind. Sinking into the water up to her neck, Pippa closed her eyes and tried to smooth out the deep frown which was scored between her eyebrows. Her head throbbed and her neck and shoulders felt stiff and sore.

If she let Steve Grainger upset her like this, it

would ruin her shot at playing Molly Brown. That would be like allowing him to violate her all over again. *Not this time*, she vowed. She had allowed Steve Grainger to ruin her life once, never again.

After her bath, Pippa put on her pyjamas and wrapped herself in an old bathrobe. Making a mug of milky coffee, she switched on the television set.

'Shit!' she spat as Steve Grainger's face filled the screen during the opening credits of his show.

Leaping up, Pippa jabbed at the buttons on the TV to change the channel. She froze as she heard someone knocking on the door to the flat.

Come on, it could be anyone. One of Alex's friends. It can't be him! Her heart was pounding in her chest as she stared at the door. The knocking started again, more insistently this time and Pippa was suddenly filled with a rage so all-consuming that she could barely see straight. Galvanised into action, she flew at the door and yanked it open.

'Leave me alone, you bastard!' she screeched, preparing to fly at him with all the force of five years pent-up emotion.

'Steady!'

Pippa stopped in her tracks, her vision clearing as she realised that it was not Steve Grainger standing on her doorstep, but a somewhat startled-looking Matt Jordan.

'You!'

Matt gave her grin that made him look quite boyish. 'Yes. Not the person you were expecting, I trust!'

Pippa shook her head, feeling foolish. Seeing his

eyes rove casually over her, she suddenly became aware of her appearance and clutched at the two sides of her bathrobe, drawing them closer together at her throat.

'I wasn't expecting anyone, actually,' she said, her voice small. 'What are you doing here?' She flushed as she realised how rude she sounded. 'I mean—'

'I know what you mean,' Matt said, rescuing her. 'I'm sorry to call round without warning like this but . . . well, I know it might sound kind of crazy since we've only just met, but I was worried about you. You seemed . . . upset when you left.'

Pippa stared at him. Had he really come all the way across town just to check that she was all right? It suddenly struck her, quite irrelevantly, she felt, that he really was incredibly attractive with his clear blue eyes sparkling merrily at her, the deep creases radiating out from them adding to rather than detracting from his appeal.

'I . . . I'm all right,' she stammered through lips that had suddenly grown dry.

'Do you think I might come in? Just for a coffee,' he added hastily when he saw the alarm chase across her features.

'Well, I—'

'It would be good to have some company for a while – it gets lonely, living in a hotel.'

He gave her his most winning smile, and Pippa felt herself relenting. After all, though she found him attractive, she had no sense of being threatened by him. She smiled somewhat shyly at him.

'Of course,' she said, stepping aside to let him in.

As he passed her, she caught a brief waft of the scent of his skin, clean and masculine. Without realising what she was doing, Pippa breathed in deeply, stunned by the sense of familiarity the odour evoked.

'Pippa?'

Matt was standing in the living-room, looking back at her with a quizzical expression on his face. There was something else too, which Pippa recognised as she gazed back at him. A reflection of her own confused emotions: desire mixed with a sense of recognition so powerful it was all she could do not to cover the short distance between them and enfold him in her arms.

'You feel it too, don't you?' he whispered, an expression of wonder crossing his features.

'What?' Pippa took a step backwards, her arms reaching round her upper body so that she was hugging herself, warding him off. Her eyes widened as he moved towards her.

'There's something ... between us,' he said. 'Something I can't describe. A feeling ... as if we've met before.'

'I don't know what you mean!' Pippa could feel the panic begin to roll over her as she stepped back again and came up against the wall. If he chose to continue to move towards her, she would be trapped between the wall and his body ...

'Pippa?'

He had stopped and was looking at her now

with a mixture of concern and puzzlement.

'Please don't come any closer.' She had to force the words through stiff lips for she was shaking now, both with the tension of the moment and the bad memories which assailed her every time a man invaded her personal space. 'Please.'

Matt recognised the odd desperation in her eyes and instinctively stepped back. Though she didn't seem to be aware of it, she had raised one hand as if to hold him off and her shoulders had hunched over protectively, as if she expected him to force himself on her. What was painfully obvious was that it was not so much him personally who had frightened her, but the situation in which she found herself.

'Pippa . . . it's all right.' Instinctively he spoke softly, backing away from her until he was by the sofa, giving her space. 'Let me make the coffee,' he suggested.

There was no response. Though she was staring at him, he had the impression that she wasn't really looking at him at all. Matt was taken aback by the intensity of the emotion he felt as he looked at her. Never before had he felt such a protective urge, such a desire to make a woman his own and cherish her. It was clear that she had been hurt at some time, by someone, and the strength of the anger that caused in him took his breath away.

She looked so vulnerable, her endearingly shabby dressing gown clutched tightly round her, her glorious red hair long and loose, lying like a shawl of spun gold around her shoulders. Her skin was pale and only very lightly freckled, as if someone had loaded a brush with gold dust and swept it swiftly across her face from left to right. Her luminous eyes, dark blue like his own, reflected extreme emotion, the depth of which he could only imagine.

From the moment she had appeared in the spotlight on the stage of the Connaught, Matt had known there was something special about her. Now he found himself aching for her, not only sexually, but with a far deeper emotion than that. It was something he had never experienced before and it bewildered as much as it excited him. For the first time in his adult life, he didn't know what to do. So he waited, allowing the silence to lengthen between them as Pippa slowly came back to him.

'I . . . I'm sorry, I . . . '

'It's all right,' he assured her hastily, feeling her embarrassment as if it was his own. Then, reluctantly, he asked, 'Would you prefer me to go?'

'Yes. Please.'

The alacrity with which she took him up on his offer cut him to the quick, so much so that he was unable to suppress the flash of pain that must have shown itself in his eyes, for she took a step towards him, her expression anguished.

'I'm sorry. It's just that I wasn't expecting anyone . . . ' It was a feeble excuse which trailed away to hang between them in the ensuing silence.

'I should have called first,' Matt said, resorting to social convention to smooth the awkwardness which had sprung between them.

What he wanted to do was ask her, *what happened to you? Who put that awful blankness in your eyes?* Instead, he turned and made for the door. As he reached it, he looked back at her.

'I'd like to take you out for dinner one evening, if I may,' he asked her formally.

For a moment he thought she was going to agree. He felt crushed as she shook her head.

'That's very kind of you, but I don't date the people I work with. It makes life too complicated.'

Their eyes met and Matt saw that she realised he knew she was lying, that her reason was an excuse rather than a truth. Realising he didn't know her well enough to challenge her, and not wanting to see that awful, haunted look in her eyes again, Matt forced himself to retreat gracefully.

'I'll see you tomorrow,' he said, opening the door to the flat.

'Yes. Matt?' He turned back to see her smile the first really genuine smile she had ever given him. It lit up her face and took his breath away. 'Thank you . . . for taking the trouble to see that I was all right.'

He returned the smile. 'Any time. Damsels in distress a speciality.' He forced himself to sound flippant, but as he closed the door he carried with him the image of that smile, and he knew that, whatever the ultimate cost, he had to have her . . .

On the stairs he bumped into an exotic-looking creature dressed from top to toe in shades of orange. He stood back to let her pass, but she seemed determined to block his way.

'Matt Jordan!'

Matt's heart sank as he was recognised, especially as this woman seemed to think he should know who she was too.

'I'm Alex,' she told him, 'I'm dancing in your new show. You weren't looking for me, were you?'

'Er, no . . . should I have been?'

He recognised the predatory gleam in the girl's eye and sighed inwardly. He wasn't in the mood for this right now. All he wanted to do was carry the image of Pippa's smile back to the hotel with him so that he could mull over their curious encounter.

'It's just that you've been to my flat.'

'Your flat? Oh, I see. Do you live with Pippa Brooks?'

'You've been to see *Pippa*?'

'Yeah. She seemed upset earlier, during rehearsal.'

Alex made a dismissive gesture. 'Pip's a bit odd like that,' she said flippantly.

Matt had to battle with his conscience before giving in to the urge to try to find out more about Pippa. Deliberately he turned on the charm.

'Do you have time for a coffee?'

Alex grinned happily. 'Sure. There's a great little tapas bar just around the corner that's open till late. Follow me.' She skipped down the stairs in front of him, making no secret of the fact that she was as pleased as punch that he had asked her.

In truth, it crossed Alexandra's mind that Matt's

interest in her stemmed primarily from his curiosity about Pippa, but her natural egotism quickly asserted itself and she disregarded the idea almost as soon as she thought it. Still feeling deliciously replete after the long, lusty hours she had spent with Frankie, she was in no mood for seduction. Not one to pass up an opportunity when it presented itself, though, Alex concentrated on laying the foundations of the relationship she hoped to develop with Matt.

Every time he asked about Pippa, Alex answered him briefly whilst managing to deflect his interest back to herself at the same time.

'Of course,' she said over coffee, 'I hope one day to climb out of the chorus, but I'm happy where I am for now. Just being a part of the production is such a thrill!'

Matt watched her animated face as she talked and realised that she was lying. Alexandra Abbott was an opportunist and she saw in him the opportunity to advance herself in the production. Fair enough, Matt thought to himself. I'll allow you to use me a little, just so long as you tell me what I want to know. Overcome with impatience, he broke into Alex's animated monologue.

'Is Pippa involved with anyone?'

Alex stopped mid-sentence and looked at him coolly.

'I'm sorry, Matt,' she said, sounding far from sorry, 'but you don't stand a chance with Pippa. She doesn't date, full stop. Actually, I'm beginning to wonder if she might not prefer girls, if you know what I mean.'

Matt stared at her, a frown drawing his brows together. Pippa, gay? That didn't gel with the impression he had gained of her so far. Yet Alex actually lived with her – maybe she was right?

'Alex—'

'Excuse me a minute, Matt – I just need to visit the little girls' room.'

Matt watched her as she leapt up and disappeared into the gloomy inner reaches of the bar. She was a strange girl, no doubt about it. Attractive enough, but curiously watchful, as if she was constantly alert to any opportunity that might present itself.

She was in the ladies' for longer than Matt had expected.

He began to feel restless, uneasy in such a public place. He had been lucky that, so far, no one had recognised him, for when they did, such situations had a habit of gaining momentum so that he was invariably forced to retreat. Sitting in a tapas bar at eleven at night with a beautiful girl would have been impossible in LA, but then the British were generally more reserved in their adulation than the Americans.

When Alex returned to the table, she smiled brightly at him, looking pleased with herself.

'Do you think you'll enjoy playing in *Chrysalis*?' she asked him as she sat down.

'It's a good script,' he said guardedly, aware that there was something about Alex he did not quite trust.

'It must be fun to work with Diana again – weren't you and she an item once?'

Matt felt uncomfortable. 'According to the tabloids,' he muttered darkly. 'Is that where you read about us?'

'Well, you have to read them if you want to know what's going on in our business, don't you?' Alex replied, unabashed.

'Do you?' It was all right for an aspiring actress to read the reports and feel she was in the know, it was quite another thing to be the person everyone was reading about, Matt thought sourly.

Alex changed the subject again and began to chatter brightly about a film she wanted to see at the cinema.

'I think I'm going to have to go on my own, though – none of my friends are into arthouse movies.'

As a prompt it couldn't have been more blatant, Matt thought cynically. If he saw her again, though, he might learn more about Pippa. Aware that he was being just as manipulative as Alex, he said, 'I'll take you, if you like.'

'Would you? That'd be terrific. How about tomorrow? Could you pick me up? That'd give me time to get home after rehearsal and improve on nature.' She fluttered her eyelashes at him and seemed disappointed when Matt didn't offer a standard compliment. With a small shrug, she told him, 'The film starts at seven-thirty.'

'Sure.' Matt wondered if it was such a good idea for Pippa to know he was taking her flatmate to the cinema. She could easily think that, having been refused by her, he had immediately turned his attentions to Alex. 'Hang on,' he said, 'I forgot – I have an appointment with my agent after rehearsal tomorrow. It might take some time. Could we meet at the cinema at seven-fifteen?'

Alex looked disappointed. 'Oh. Okay. Well, I'd better be getting back – I'm bushed! See you tomorrow.'

'Yeah. Hang on, I'll walk you to your block.'

Alex smiled at him and as they walked out of the restaurant together, she slipped her hand through his arm. Matt was suddenly aware of her perfume and the softness of her breast pressing against his upper arm. Glancing at her, he saw her eyes narrow seductively as she looked up at him, and he wondered what she was playing at.

Suddenly from his right there was a blinding flash as a photographer appeared from nowhere. Recognising him at once as the staff photographer from *The Record*, the tabloid with whom he had had a running battle in the courts as well as in his private life, Matt swore and pushed the man aside, pulling Alex after him.

'Bloody parasites!' he seethed as he ran across the road and rounded the corner. 'I'm sorry about that, Alex,' he said as they reached the building which housed her flat. 'Would you mind if I dash now? If you go straight up, that moron should leave you alone.'

'Of course. I'll see you tomorrow, Matt.'

Alex watched as he walked swiftly away and

got into his car, which was parked further down the street. Lingering outside, she made sure that the reporter who had been with the photographer saw her outside her block of flats before pretending to fumble with the door.

'Hey! Hold on a minute, love – would you mind answering a few questions?'

The man was puffing, his shiny pink pate glistening under the light of the street-lamp as he drew level with her. The light reflected off his glasses, lending a satanic cast to his otherwise round and inoffensive-looking features.

'Are you all right?' Alex asked sweetly.

'I will be in a minute.' The man took out a clean white handkerchief and mopped his face with it. 'Would you like to tell me your name?' he asked after he'd put it away and pulled out his notebook.

'We-ell—'

'I'll find out eventually anyway, love,' he said, cutting off Alex's feigned protest.

Affecting a shy smile, she made sure the photographer got a few good shots of her as he caught up with the reporter.

'All right. I guess everyone will know eventually anyway. My name is Alexandra Abbott. That's two "bees", two "tees". I'm a dancer in Matt's new show.'

'Have you two been seeing each other for long?'

Alex dropped her eyes and gazed up at him through her lashes coyly.

'Not long, no.'

'You wouldn't happen to know who tipped off the paper that you were out together, would you?'

The photographer, who had remained silent up to now, cut in.

Alexandra looked at him steadily. He was an attractive man with thick, unruly black hair, dressed in serviceable denim. His skin was olive-toned and very smooth and his dark brown eyes challenged her even while they glittered with amusement. Alex smiled slowly.

'I have no idea,' she said coolly.

'Really?' There was cynicism in the photographer's smile.

Turning her back dismissively on the other man, Alex leaned forward so that she was mere inches away from him.

'What's your name?' she asked.

'Oliver Leeder. Two "ees",' he mocked her gently.

Alex smiled. Reaching out, she ran her forefinger under the strap of his camera as it hung around his neck.

'Nice kit,' she murmured, feeling the warmth of his skin through his shirt on the backs of her fingers.

'It does the job.'

His voice was low and confident and he was looking at her as if he thought he had her measure. Alex liked his arrogance, knowing she could break it down in no time and have him eating out of her hand. For all Matt Jordan's film-star looks and raw masculinity, she found Oliver Leeder by far the more interesting of the two men.

She could sense the tension in his limbs as she

toyed with him. In other circumstances, she would have invited him upstairs – she knew he wouldn't refuse her. A photographer of his standing could be very useful to her. For now, though, she had bigger fish to fry, so she reluctantly put him on hold.

'I have to go up now,' she said, and with a final smile at the gentlemen of the press, she shut the door in their faces.

Pippa could not believe her eyes when she went to the newsagent's the following morning and saw the front page of the *The Record*. The photograph of Alex and Matt took up half the page, the headlines blaring: MATT'S NEW GIRL. Matt was holding up his hand to shield his face, but Alex was caught gazing adoringly at him, happy, it seemed, for all the world to know who she was with. And why not? Pippa thought savagely. Matt Jordan was quite a catch for an aspiring actress like Alexandra Abbott.

It was normally Alex who bought *The Record* – Pippa couldn't raise enough interest in the goings-on of the rich and famous which was all that seemed to make up the 'news' – but today she shoved it into her basket with the milk and bread and hurried back to the flat.

Alex virtually snatched the paper from her when she walked through the door.

'Wow! Great picture, eh, Pip? And they even spelt my name right!' She laughed.

'When did you go out with Matt, Alex?' Pippa asked, aware that she felt hurt and used. Had Matt been looking for Alex when he called in last night? If so he certainly had her fooled, she thought bitterly. To think she had thought that he genuinely cared that she had been upset! Alexandra's next words only served to confuse her further.

'I bumped into him as he left here last night. You moved fast, Pippa, I'll grant you that, but you obviously didn't follow through, which left the way wide open for me.' Alex's grin was smug and Pippa frowned.

'What do you mean?'

'Oh, come on, Pip! Matt said he had been to see you – some crap about thinking you were upset about something. Good line, that – appeal to the macho protective streak. I'll have to try that myself someday. Anyhow, *one* of us got a plug out of it, didn't we?'

Pippa stared at Alex in confusion. Did she really think that Pippa had been trying to garner favours from Matt? That she was looking for publicity to give her career a boost? Realising that she did think exactly that, it dawned on Pippa that she really didn't know her flatmate very well at all.

'Do you mean to say you organised all this?' she said, gesturing at the paper.

Alex looked pleased with herself. 'Sure. A quick phone call to *The Record* to let them know that Matt Jordan was out with his new girl, and Bob's your uncle!'

Pippa was shocked. 'Did Matt know about this?'

'What do you think?' Alex replied witheringly.

Pippa looked at the photograph again. While

Alex was posing blatantly for the camera, Matt looked far removed from someone who was looking for publicity. Glancing up at Alex, she felt a sharp stab of dislike for her.

'Alex . . . that's despicable! You used Matt just to get your name in the paper. How could you do that to him?'

Alex shrugged and picked up the paper.

'Easy, baby. Matt Jordan might be known for hating publicity, but then he doesn't need it, does he? C'mon, Pip,' she said, impatience colouring her every word, 'wise up. No one gets on in this business if they're not prepared to court the press. Matt might *pretend* that he doesn't like their attention, but, let's face it, he does all right out of their interest, doesn't he? Never mind the publicity, look at the size of the settlement he got from *The Record* last time he brought a suit for libel against them. I'll bet he and his agent scour every newspaper looking for a phrase they can object to!'

Pippa felt appalled by Alex's attitude. 'People get hurt by things like this. Supposing Matt was involved with someone – it would be humiliating for him to have been photographed like this.'

Alex shrugged, unmoved by Pippa's indignation. 'Well, he's not, is he?'

'But that's not the point – ' Pippa broke off as she saw that Alex was barely listening to her. 'What will he say when he sees this? He could sack you from the show!'

'Oh Pippa, don't be so prim! He's not going to sack me. In fact, he's taking me out tonight. Now,

I'm going back to bed to read all about myself. See you later!'

She stalked out of the room, leaving Pippa aghast, outraged on Matt's behalf. *But no one was forcing him to take Alex out tonight*, she told herself. And Alex was clever enough to feign innocence about the tip-off to the press. Most men were pretty stupid when it came to Alex – why should Matt Jordan be any different?

For some reason the idea thoroughly depressed her.

Chapter Five

TWO WEEKS BEFORE Chrysalis was due to open, Steve Grainger stood on the sidelines and watched as Pippa rehearsed her main scene with Matt Jordan. She had always been good, even while they were at drama college, but there was no mistaking her star quality now.

'What makes you think you can buy me?' her character was saying to Matt's.

Matt Jordan smiled that raffish, mega-dollar smile and caught at her arm.

'Everyone has their price,' he opined, pulling her into his arms.

Steve watched as Pippa twined her arms around his neck and allowed her head to fall back in order to look into his eyes. She was able to convey the challenge that would be in them to the watching audience, just as Matt gave the impression of desire barely held in check.

There was a chemistry between the two actors which attracted the rest of the cast. They all watched in silence as the scene was played out, collectively willing the couple to move into the kiss.

Steve watched Pippa's face. Every time she played this scene a kind of blankness settled over her features which infuriated Lee Broadbent. It was descending now, but this time Matt did not give her eyes the time to glaze over, he kissed her quickly, holding her by the back of the head so that she couldn't pull away and attract the director's ire once again.

Watching, Steve felt his cock stir. The memory of her squirming in his arms was all too vivid. His eyes ran down Pippa's body, remembering what she had looked like naked. She was thinner now, with a kind of edgy restlessness in her limbs which meant she seemed to be constantly in motion. Her skin had been very white, very soft, and he guessed that would not have changed. He remembered her perfume . . . something light and floral . . . *Anaïs Anaïs*, that was it. Strange, he imagined he could smell it now . . .

'What are the chances of her getting it right, do you think?'

He turned to see Diana George watching the couple on stage with a sour expression on her face. Steve's mind scrolled back until he recalled the rumours about her and Matt Jordan some years before and he smiled to himself.

'She's certainly making a meal of it, isn't she?' he agreed, turning the full force of his smile on the older woman.

Diana blinked, her attention forced away from

the spectacle of Matt kissing the other actress. Steve recognised her attitude change as she looked him up and down assessingly.

'How are you enjoying your foray into theatre?' she asked him.

'It's very . . interesting,' he replied, moving closer to her. 'It's good to work with professionals such as yourself.'

Diana smiled cynically. 'Flattery, darling, will get you everywhere! Have you finished for the day?'

Recognising the gleam of sexual arousal in her eye, Steve glanced back at the stage. His jaw tightened as he saw that the couple were still kissing, still pressing closely together, apparently oblivious to the other actors, the director, and even the time.

Turning back to Diana, he ran his eyes over her assessingly. According to her publicity, she was in her mid-forties, which probably meant she was fifty, at least, Steve thought cynically. Still, she had worn well and was not afraid to enlist the aid of a plastic surgeon when required to keep her on the 'A' list of desirable actresses.

From the way she was looking at him now, her famous lavender-blue eyes luminescent and her full, collagen-pumped lips moist, slightly parted to show neat, white teeth, Steve guessed that her famous libido was as rapacious as ever. Why not respond to the blatant come-on?

'It looks like it,' he said, replying to her question at last.

Diana smiled slowly at him and Steve felt the

first genuine stab of lust for her as she leaned closer to him.

'Your place or mine?' she asked huskily.

Steve thought of his stark, modern flat, all glass and monochromic style and suppressed a shudder at the thought of sullying its perfection with anything as textural as a woman's naked body. His home was his sanctuary, his impregnable lair and he never, ever allowed anyone to visit him there.

'Yours,' he said, making it sound as though he was doing her a favour. 'It's nearer.'

'How do you know that?' she said, laughing.

'It's bound to be.'

Without another backward glance at the scene being enacted on the stage behind him, Steve took Diana by the elbow and they left the theatre together.

Pippa stared at Matt, her eyes wide and uncomprehending as, at last, he let her go. Her lips burned where his had been, the entire length of her body still conscious of the imprint of his against it. His eyes seemed to bore into her, looking into her mind as he stared unblinkingly at her.

'Thank you – I think that's rehearsal enough.' The director's voice cut into her thoughts, making her conscious that they were not alone as, for those few, unreal moments, she had imagined that they were.

She felt curiously abandoned as they parted and she turned away, sensing Matt watching her as she left the stage. He hadn't said a word, yet Pippa felt the kiss he had all but forced on her had been more eloquent than any words could be.

As she forced herself to walk, rather than run as her instincts wanted her to, off the stage, she passed Alexandra. Alex stared at her without smiling and Pippa felt a chill pass through her as she recognised the hostility in the other girl's eyes. Not understanding, she opened her mouth to say something, but Alex turned away, leaving Pippa to make her way back to the dressing-room alone.

As she changed, she relived the scene she had been rehearsing. Five, six times, Matt had tried to kiss her as the script demanded. Each time, Pippa had felt herself freeze, her arms and legs growing leaden, her mind retreating from the physical reality of the act.

Lee Broadbent had been scathing, flogging her verbally at each failed attempt. The more she tried, and failed, the more desperate she felt, until she was convinced that she was going to be hauled off the stage, her career in tatters. An actress who was unable to kiss an actor? What use would she be? Then Matt had taken her by surprise, capturing her mouth with his before she had the chance to erect her defences, and in those few moments, everything had changed.

At first, she had pulled back, instinctively recoiling from the feeling of his warm lips against hers. Matt reacted by putting his hand at the back of her head and holding her still. Panic, sharp and frightening, had ripped through her, yet she hadn't succumbed to it, reaching instead for the elusive sensation of joy that being close to him evoked in her.

Stronger than the memories of revulsion and pain, more insistent than the need to protect herself, a deep, satisfying pleasure seemed to trickle, syrup-like, through her veins. Their surroundings seemed to shift out of focus, as if they had been shifted onto a separate timeline, away from everybody else where only they existed, where their kiss was the only reality.

Bringing her fingers up to her lips, Pippa realised that her hand was trembling. Her stomach churned and her head was spinning with a confusion of thoughts. Since his visit to her flat, Matt had maintained a friendly distance, understandable since he was now dating Alexandra on a regular basis.

Alex. No wonder the other girl had been so hostile; it must have been clear to anyone with eyes in their head that the kiss went far beyond the mechanics required for the smooth telling of the play's story! Pippa put her hands over her eyes and groaned. What had she been thinking of? Allowing herself to be carried away when—

'Pippa?'

She spun round as Matt appeared in the doorway.

'What? What do you want?'

He seemed taken aback by her agitation.

'Pippa, we have to talk—'

'What about?' she interrupted him aggressively, not wanting to listen to what he had to say.

'About us . . . what happened just now.'

Steadying herself, Pippa forced the actress in her to the fore. 'It'll be a good scene, won't it?'

Matt's eyes looked bleak and it was all she could do not to run to him.

'Yes,' he said, his voice flat and emotionless, 'it will. It was just that I thought—'

'What? What did you think, Matt?'

He shook his head. 'Nothing. See you at tonight's party, Pippa.'

Of course, she'd forgotten that Jason Duval, the play's major backer, was throwing a party for the production crew and cast. Everyone was expected to attend and most were looking forward to it. The way she felt right now, it sounded to Pippa like a form of exquisite torture, watching Matt with Alex whilst trying to avoid Steve.

'Yes,' she said now, 'of course.'

Matt closed the door quietly behind him, leaving Pippa in turmoil.

Steve looked around Diana's classy Knightsbridge flat and wrinkled his nose in distaste. What a tip! There were magazines strewn haphazardly across the sofa, clothing draped carelessly across the backs of the chairs. He tripped on a high-heeled shoe which had been left in the middle of the floor. Ashtrays overflowed on every surface and some half a dozen cats stalked territorially about the living-room. One casually raked its claws down the arm of the pale pink, leather sofa, adding to the trammel lines already scored there.

'Find a seat while I pour us a drink,' Diana said, waving one exquisitely manicured hand towards the sofa.

Glancing at the old newspapers and letters piled up on the cushions, Steve opted instead to walk over to the elegant, narrow sash windows on the far side of the room.

'Have you lived here long?' he asked her without any real interest.

'A while. Here.'

She passed him a glass – Scotch, he noticed, and she hadn't even asked him – and he mustered a polite smile. What the hell was he doing here with this predatory, sluttish old tart?

He watched as Diana threw back her head and downed her Scotch in one.

'Well,' she said in a businesslike tone as she put her glass down amidst countless others on a side table, 'there's nothing like afternoon delight! Let's go through to the bedroom, shall we?'

Steve put his untouched glass down next to hers and followed her into her bedroom.

At seven o'clock, Matt found himself still at the Connaught as the backer made his welcome speech. An old friend of Matt's, Jason Duval liked to make up for his own lack of thespian talent by using part of the fortune he had made in computer software to invest in the London theatre scene.

'I just want you all to know that I'm proud of you all, that I am, and I just know that *Chrysalis* is gonna be the biggest hit since . . . the last biggest hit!'

Everyone laughed dutifully. Jason, East End boy made good with no illusions about why he appeared to have so many friends in the room, gave Matt a wink.

'There's loadsa nosh on the side there, and booze. Anyone who wants wild sex can come back to my place after. Bums up!'

Matt scanned the room as the buzz of conversation swelled again after Jason's small speech. He frowned as he realised that there was still no sign of Pippa. Since she'd made it so abundantly clear earlier that she wanted nothing to do with him, he'd decided that he could do without the hassle of trying to change her mind. After all, there were plenty of others to take her place. Alexandra, for example, who, after the fiasco with *The Record*, had become a convenient companion. Though he didn't quite trust her, he had to admit that she was amusing company. Dating Alex also had the useful effect of keeping Diana at bay, an advantage for which Matt was truly grateful.

Forgetting Pippa, though, had turned out to be more difficult than he thought and as time had gone on he was slowly coming the conclusion that the bond he sensed between them was no mere figment of his imagination, but something very real. For him, the kiss they had shared only strengthened that conviction, for it was like no other kiss he had ever shared with a woman.

If he closed his eyes, he could still feel the shape of her body, the way she had trembled, her limbs vibrating with a reaction he didn't quite understand. Holding her had felt so good, so utterly right, he could have stood with her like that all afternoon. But what could he do? Pippa clearly didn't feel the same – quite the opposite.

He forced a congenial grin now as Jason made his way over.

'Good party, Jason,' he said.

Opening another bottle of champagne, Jason looked around him with satisfaction.

'Not bad, eh? I like the look of your bird,' he said, nodding at Alex who was talking animatedly to Lee Broadbent. 'Is it serious?'

Matt shook his head. 'If I let on to Alex that you're more influential in this production than I am, she'll be all over you like a rash.'

'Doesn't seem to bother you, mate.'

'No, it doesn't,' Matt admitted. He felt ineffably weary. What the hell was he doing dating someone he didn't particularly care about? He couldn't even claim that he felt closer to Pippa when he was with Alex, for the two clearly weren't as close as he had hoped they would be.

'Got someone else in your sights?' Jason asked with characteristic shrewdness.

'In a way, yes.'

'So what's the problem?'

Matt shrugged. 'She's not interested.'

Jason grimaced. 'I wouldn't waste your time, mate, if I was you. There're plenty of women out there.'

'Not like this one,' Matt said with a conviction that surprised him. Maybe he should disregard their unsatisfactory conversation earlier and pursue Pippa with a little more determination. Realising that Jason was watching him, he made a small, self-deprecating gesture.

'You've got it bad, mate,' his old friend said, in a tone which implied he'd picked up some kind of social disease. 'Looks to me like you're on your way out of the carefree bachelor club. We'll be gutted to lose you.' He sucked in his breath over his teeth and shook his head sorrowfully, making Matt laugh.

'I don't think it's that bad.'

'No? Come back to my place later, then. Bring your bird, if you like. I've got some decent girls coming – know what I mean?'

Matt rolled his eyes. Jason was incorrigible. Matt knew exactly what would go on at his party. Once upon a time, he too would have been game for anything. Now, though, he seemed to have lost all desire for other women.

'What's Alex like in the sack?' Jason asked bluntly.

Matt followed his gaze to where Alexandra was flirting with one of the male dancers. Dressed in shades of orange and scarlet, she was like an exotic bird of paradise strutting restlessly around her territory. On anyone else the floaty top and tight-fitting tube of a long skirt which reached her ankles, skimming the tops of her silver mock-snakeskin Doc Martens, would have looked ill-matched, ridiculous even. On Alex it just looked right, somehow, a reflection of her changeable, off-beat personality.

'Well?' Jason nudged him, snapping his thoughts back to the present.

'What?'

'Christ, mate, what are you on?'

Matt frowned. 'Sorry. What did you say?'

'I said, what's she like in the sack? Alex – your bird?'

'I wouldn't know.'

'What?' Jason looked at him as if he'd just confessed to crimes against humanity. 'You're trying to tell me you're not sleeping with her?'

Matt shrugged again. How could he explain to someone like Jason that there was only one woman he wanted, and that, since he'd met her, no one else would do?

Pippa treated herself to a long, hot soak and an early night on the evening of the cast party. Alex had promised to make apologies for her if she was missed and Pippa trusted her to do so. Alex certainly didn't want her anywhere near Matt and after what had happened between them this afternoon . . .

She felt a pang of anguish as she considered how he had kept at arm's length since he'd started dating Alex. It was hard, seeing him every day and knowing how she had put a halt to their friendship before it had even begun. It didn't help when Alex regaled her with lurid stories about his sexual prowess, returning home after each date with a satisfied grin on her face.

Not that sleeping with Matt made her change the habits of a lifetime. Pippa wondered what Matt would think about the ever-changing stream of casual dates Alex continued to bring back to the flat. Maybe he behaved in exactly the same way and so wouldn't think anything of it. For some reason the idea brought her pain and so she pushed it forcefully away.

At one time, Pippa had felt quite close to Alexandra. Since they had started work on *Chrysalis*, though, she had discovered a selfish, self-promoting streak in her flatmate that she really didn't like. Eventually, she supposed, she would have to think about looking for a flat of her own. Right now, though, what with the challenge of playing Molly Brown and having to contend with Steve Grainger's spite, she simply didn't have the necessary energy spare to even think about moving.

Considering the stress she had been under since rehearsals began, Pippa found it surprisingly easy to drift into sleep. The flat was quiet without Alex and the combination of a warm bath and exhaustion conspired to draw her into the dream-world without any difficulty at all. Once there she began to dream about Matt.

In her dream, he was smiling at her, holding out his arms to welcome her as she walked towards him. Pippa turned restlessly in the bed as she was enfolded in Matt's embrace. He held her tenderly, yet his arms were strong around her. She could feel the play of muscle beneath the skin as he ran his palms down her back to rest in the dip at her waist. Pelvis to pelvis, she could feel the firm column of his penis press against the softness of her belly, not urgently or insistently, but without shame or apology.

Stepping back, Matt pulled his T-shirt over his head to reveal golden skin, his chest smooth and hairless, the nipples small and perfectly round. Reaching out, Pippa traced the outline of each one with the very tip of her fingernail, noticing how his pectorals tautened at her touch.

She could smell the familiar scent of his skin, overlaid by the warm, musky odour of masculine arousal. He was wearing casual sports trousers in a soft material which left little to the imagination. The fabric moulded the long, finely muscled length of his thighs and delineated the line of his penis.

Holding his eye, Pippa covered it with the palm of her hand and held it there, without moving. Matt's eyes closed briefly and his adam's apple bobbed in his throat as he swallowed. As if sensing her need to control the situation, he stood very still and allowed her to run her other hand over his chest and down to his stomach.

The muscles there contracted as she stroked her fingertips across them, and his cock twitched against her other hand. She could feel the heat of it through his trousers. At once, she wanted to feel his naked skin against her palm. Hooking her thumbs in the elasticated waistband of his track pants she drew them down slowly over his hips.

His penis sprang free from its constraint, knocking eagerly against her stomach. Somewhat bizarrely, she was wearing a long-sleeved dress of pale pink silk, the style of which covered her from throat to ankle. As the tip of Matt's penis brushed against it, a drop of fluid smeared the front of the dress, the wet patch spreading like a stain across her stomach.

Pippa waited until he had stepped out of the track pants and had kicked them aside. Now he stood before her, completely naked and acquiescent. She could sense the leashed tension in him and the knowledge that he was holding back for her filled her with awe.

Desire, warm and fluid, trickled through her, centring on the hidden folds at the apex of her thighs. She could feel her inner flesh swell and throb, secretly, unlike Matt's sex-flesh which reared up like a sentinel, his arousal blatant and proud.

Pippa watched Matt's face as she reached for him. A muscle spasmed in his jaw and his eyes glazed over as she wrapped her hand around the long, firm stem of his penis. It felt hot in her palm, the skin so soft over the hard core.

Slowly, as if instinctively knowing what to do, Pippa moved the loose outer skin over the shaft, causing Matt's breath to escape through his lips on a sigh. She loved the softened, unfocused look on his face as she touched him and she moved forward to brush her lips against the corner of his mouth. Matt's lips softened as she ran the tip of her tongue along the join, tasting the sweetness of his inner flesh.

It occured to her then that she knew what he wanted her to do. He didn't have to ask, or show her, and she knew instinctively that he would show no disappointment if she moved away. It was *her* dream, and he would allow her to set the pace. More surprisingly, perhaps, she realised that she wanted the same thing.

Slowly, still holding his eye, Pippa sank to her knees in front of him. From close quarters, his penis looked large and potent, its exposed tip soft and pink, shiny with the clear fluid of pre-emission. Trembling slightly, Pippa took the rigid stem and guided the tip to her lips.

His fluid smeared her lips and she snaked out her tongue to taste the warm, sea-salt flavour of it. Becoming bolder, she traced the small slit which leaked a little fresh fluid onto her tongue.

Matt touched her then, reaching down to stroke her hair. The loving gesture increased her confidence, encouraging her to go on. Stretching her lips wide, she fed the soft head of his penis into her mouth until her lips reached the ridge.

For a few seconds, she held it there, enjoying the taste and texture of the fine-skinned bulb. Flicking her tongue around the ridge, she discovered a sensitive spot on the underside, feeling rather than hearing Matt's sigh of sheer pleasure.

Slipping her hand underneath him, she stroked the smooth, swollen sac beneath his cock. In her dream, the hair covering it was soft and silky and the small balls inside seemed to swell in her hand as she cupped them gently.

Slowly she fed the rest of him into her mouth, inch by inch, until she couldn't take any more. Then she moved her head back, dragging on the loose skin with her lips, making him shiver before drawing the length of him into her mouth again.

In her bed, Pippa moved restlessly under the covers as the dream affected her. Halfway between sleep and waking, she pulled off her pyjamas and threw them aside in a vain attempt to cool herself. Her skin felt itchy and hot, her mouth becoming dry as she ran her palms feverishly over her body.

'Oh, Matt,' she murmured as her dream-self kissed and caressed him, running her hands over his thighs which trembled at her touch.

In her dream, his fingers meshed in her hair, his fingertips massaging her scalp as she sucked on him, drawing the seed from his body as if it was the sweetest, most precious nectar. And as she milked him, she was filled with the most incredible sensation, such a sense of herself as a woman that she felt herself tip over into orgasm.

It was so strong, so powerful, that it woke her completely. Wrenched into wakefulness, Pippa pressed her hand against her vulva and felt her sex-flesh throbbing, her clitoris pulsing with life. For a moment she was confused, not knowing if she was awake or still dreaming.

It didn't matter. Closing her eyes, she welcomed the sensations still travelling through her, pressing the heel of her hand against her pubic bone to prolong the ripples of pleasure. In her mind's eye, she saw Matt as he had looked earlier that afternoon, tasted again the sweetness of his lips as they moved on hers, and felt herself filled with an aching yearning that brought tears to her eyes.

As her climax finally began to ebb away, Pippa wrapped herself in the duvet tightly. In the soft, forgiving darkness, she reviewed her dream. The detail both shocked and thrilled her. That she could be capable of such a response during an encounter which was marked by the complete absence of fear seemed incredible to her. The only real drawback was that the object of her fantasies was Matt Jordan, and he seemed to have lost interest in her all too quickly.

Telling herself that the important thing was that her body was capable of responding in such a way to a mere dream, Pippa slept, at last, and this time her sleep was deep and dreamless.

Chapter Six

STEVE WATCHED AS Diana walked, naked, into the bathroom. Her body was smooth and flawless, all the nips and tucks for which she was famous cleverly concealed. Making love to her had been like bonking a plastic blow-up doll – Diana's lovemaking style was as expressionless as it was efficient.

He waited until she came back out of the bathroom. Her make-up had been renewed and she'd brushed her hair so that she looked as if she'd just walked, naked, out of the beauty salon. Picking up her slim gold watch from the bedside table, she glanced at the luminous face.

'Isn't it time we got ready for Jason's party?' she suggested.

'In a minute. Come here.'

Steve watched Diana's face as she walked over to the bed. He knew her type – though she cultivated the persona of a love goddess, she didn't actually like sex. Inviting him back to her place had been something she felt compelled to do, as if she needed to continually renew her own image of herself as a desirable woman.

'Sit down.' He made his voice dark and persuasive, watching her carefully for any reaction.

There was none and, for a moment, he thought about leaving. Then she glanced over at the dressing-table and, catching sight of her reflection in the mirror, she smoothed back her already perfectly styled hair.

That one small act of vanity sent a shiver of familiar sensation coursing through Steve's veins. Here was a woman for whom attraction and seduction came as naturally as eating and sleeping, yet who, at her heart, was as empty as a pearlless oyster shell. She was a Barbie-doll, a walking-talking fuck-machine.

An image of Pippa kissing Matt Jordan seared through his mind, coating everything he saw in a fine red mist. His heart began to pound in his chest and sweat pushed its way through his pores. Breathing was painful, his lungs aching in his chest as he allowed rationality to slip away.

'Now let's see what you can really do,' he said, reaching for Diana.

Something about the tone of his voice warned Diana of imminent danger, but it was far, far too late. She tried to pull away from hands that had become rough and careless, but Steve was too strong, and too determined. That he was determined to use her however he saw fit was plain, and her protests fell on deaf ears, her struggles only serving to make him angry.

Desperately, Diana imagined herself in a film, in a role more real and gritty than she had ever played before. *This is not me*, she told herself, *this is not happening to me*. Her lips drew back from her teeth in a parody of a grin, a rictus of fear and pain.

Blanking her mind from the horror she knew was to come, Diana withdrew from reality, going inside herself to a place where no one could hurt her.

Close to midnight, Steve arrived at the cast party alone. He was still edgy, his body buzzing with adrenalin. Things had gone a little too far with Diana, he realised that. If only she hadn't given him that stupid, inane grin . . . he shrugged. She'd get over it. So what if things had got a bit rough between them? She'd been round the block a few times – he was willing to bet she wasn't nearly as shocked as she'd made out. Too bad she hadn't wanted to come with him to the party. Once they got going, they'd had some fun. He smiled to himself.

Inside, he was soon surrounded by a multitude of starry-eyed wannabes and quickly decided he was quite glad Diana had elected to stay away after all.

'Come and dance with me, Steve,' a young, breathy voice said in his ear. Turning, he saw a short, fluffy-haired blonde whom he was sure he had never seen before. She didn't look more than sixteen, though the way she pressed up against him was far from innocent. Why not give her a thrill?

'Sure,' he said, treating her to the smile he reserved for adoring fans, 'lead the way, baby.'

She led, her ample, rounded buttocks fighting each other for space beneath the tight, Lycra seat of her cycle shorts, and he followed.

Matt and Alex had barely spent five minutes together all evening. Watching her from across the room, Matt found himself comparing her unfavourably with Pippa. It wasn't fair to do so, he knew that, but he couldn't help himself.

'Is that the girl?'

He jumped as Moira appeared at his elbow and nodded towards Alex. He'd told her earlier he'd met someone special, so it was understandable that she'd assumed it must be Alexandra.

'Good God, no!' he replied, unable to suppress a shudder. Alex – the girl of his dreams? It didn't bear thinking about!

Moira chuckled softly. 'Thank heavens for that!' she said, taking another glass of wine from a passing waitress.

'What makes you say that?' Matt asked curiously.

'*That* girl is in love with herself – you need someone a little deeper than that. Someone who's more than one-dimensional.'

'Do I?' Matt smiled affectionately at her. 'You'd like Pippa, she's anything but one-dimensional.'

'Where is she?' Moira scanned the room, as if she might be able to recognise Pippa simply because Matt had confessed to being more than a little in love with her.

'She's not here.'

'Oh? Why not?'

Matt shrugged. 'I don't know.'

'I see. Can I ask you a question, Matt, as one old friend to another?'

Matt threw her a pained glance. 'What gives me the feeling I'm not going to like this?' Ignoring him, Moira fixed him with her steady gaze. 'What are you doing here with that girl,' she gestured towards Alex, 'when you obviously would rather be with someone else?'

Matt held her eye and sighed heavily. 'Could it be that I'm a spineless, cowardly, two-timing bastard?' he asked before she could rail at him.

She smiled, allowing herself to be partially disarmed. 'Could be,' she agreed. 'Or maybe you're scared.'

'*Scared?*'

'Aha! No slick answer this time. Yes, Matt – *scared*. You've never had to handle rejection before, have you, not like most of us mortals. Maybe the fact that this Pippa isn't so eager to fall at your feet has brought you face to face with your own resistibility.'

There was a thread of bitterness in her words that cut Matt to the quick.

'Why do I get the impression that you think I'm getting my just deserts?'

Moira smiled and put her hand on his arm.

'I don't, Matt,' she said gently. 'I'm your friend, remember? That's what gives me the right to say things you don't want to hear. Maybe I'm talking out of my hat – after all, I've never even met Pippa. But she's clearly made an impression on you. Isn't she worth risking a blow to your ego to see if there could be something between you?'

Reaching up, she planted a kiss on his cheek before moving briskly away. Matt watched her weave her way towards Brad, who was fending off the advances of a trio of fledgling actors on the look-out for an agent. He smiled as he saw Moira, welcoming her into the group with a hug.

For no particular reason, Matt felt moved by the quiet expression of love. Was Moira right – was he afraid to pursue Pippa? Her remarks about his ego had made him feel uncomfortable, for he knew they weren't entirely unjustified. He considered the view she had painted of him and realised that, at that moment, he didn't like himself very much. When Pippa hadn't instantly fallen into his arms, he'd retreated at once, blithely expecting her to come round eventually. He hadn't made any attempt to woo her, to show her how deep his feelings ran. Instead, he'd taken out her flatmate instead.

'Hell, what a rat I am!' he muttered to himself.

'Did you want something, Mr Jordan?'

He turned to see a young waitress looking at him quizzically. *Yes*, he thought to himself, *I want my head testing!* Aloud, he requested another drink, and went to find somewhere to sit down.

'We could go outside,' Steve Grainger whispered in Alexandra's ear.

Alex threw back her head and laughed. She was intoxicated by the amount of attention she had received during this party, particularly from Steve Grainger, who hadn't so much as glanced in her direction until this evening.

'I'm with Matt,' she protested unconvincingly.

Steve made a dismissive gesture with his head.

'He doesn't deserve you.'

That was true, Alex thought as she glanced over to where Matt was nursing a glass of whisky at a table. He'd been a miserable sod all evening. Come to think of it, he hadn't turned out to be half as much fun as she had expected, especially not in the bedroom department. Not that she'd ever admit that to anyone – she'd rather die than broadcast the fact that she'd found the first man ever who apparently didn't find her irresistible.

'And you *do* deserve me, I suppose,' she said to Steve, allowing herself to be charmed by his famous cheeky grin.

'I know how to give a girl a good time,' he said.

'I just bet you do!' Alex said, her voice low and husky.

Steve reached out unexpectedly and touched the tip of his finger against her breast. The nipple sprang to life at once, hardening under the clingy Lycra fabric of her top. Steve increased the pressure and Alex caught her breath as a sharp dart of pleasure pierced her belly.

'No,' she whispered, moving away reluctantly.

'C'mon, Alex – you want it, you know you do.'

He was right, she *did* want it, more than he

could imagine, but she wanted one last crack at Matt before she gave up on him.

'Not here, not now,' she said firmly.

For a moment she thought that Steve was going to sulk, but his expression quickly cleared and he shrugged.

'Okay. Let me know when you get tired of Mr Squeaky-clean and want a real man inside you.'

He moved away before Alex had time to respond, leaving her tingling inside.

'Hello, love – all alone?'

She turned to find Jason Duval standing at her elbow. His eyes travelled appreciatively over her close-fitting top, lingering on the erect nipples pressing against the fabric. Unabashed, Alex puffed out her chest and allowed it to brush against his arm as she leaned forward to make herself heard above the din.

'You give a great party, Mr Duval,' she said.

'Jason, please. This is nothing – I've been trying to persuade Matt to bring you back to my place later. That's when the fun will really begin.'

'That'd be great!' Things couldn't be better – if the backer had noticed her she might not need Matt after all to get on in this production.

'Let's go and persuade him then, shall we?'

Alex was about to protest that she was perfectly happy to come without Matt, if he didn't want to go, but she stopped herself just in time. It wouldn't do to look *too* eager. Instead, she nodded and followed Jason to the table where Matt was nursing a tumblerful of whisky over ice.

'Hi,' she said, draping herself across the back of his chair. 'Jason says we're invited to his party. Sounds like fun.'

Matt glanced up at her, then across to Jason, who was watching him with a glint of amusement in his eyes. There was a challenge there too, and Matt regretted mentioning Pippa to him. He'd had too much to drink and would far rather had gone straight back to the hotel to sleep it off, but the pressure was on now to prove himself unchanged.

'Sure, Alex,' he said with a shrug, 'we'll go if you want to.'

'I want to,' she said, as he'd known she would.

'That's settled then. You two come in my car.'

Alex smiled. The evening was going from good to incredible. In the back of Jason's chauffeur-driven Rolls, Alex sat between the two men on the soft leather seat. Matt gazed morosely out of the window, apparently oblivious to her and his surroundings. Jason, however, was more attentive.

'How do you like dancing?' he asked, eyeing the outline of her long, slender thighs which were clearly delineated by the tight tube skirt.

Alex smiled and shrugged. 'It's okay. I'm very ambitious – I don't want to be in the chorus forever!'

Jason laughed out loud. 'I admire your honesty, Alex,' he said, 'but do you have the talent to go with it?'

Fixing him with a suggestive smoulder, Alex leaned forward so that he could smell the faint, spicy scent of her perfume.

'That's for you to find out, isn't it?' she said huskily.

Jason's grey eyes darkened a fraction, his gaze flickering to her breasts, hidden beneath the voluminous folds of her floaty orange top.

'I might just do that,' he said, his voice uneven.

Alex smiled, reaching out her hand to caress his thigh. She could feel his muscles contract at her touch, hardening and bunching beneath the thin fabric of his trousers. Jason glanced past her at Matt.

'Don't mind him,' Alex whispered, 'he doesn't own me.'

Jason looked at her with faint distaste until she moved her hand, placing it quite deliberately on the tumescence in his lap. His penis engorged as she squeezed it gently, setting up a rhythm that made him feel hot and restless. Holding her eye, Jason leaned across and, copying her movement, placed his hand in her lap.

'I'm hot,' she whispered.

He could feel that she was. His cock twitched as he thought how she would feel if the barrier of her clothing was removed. Imagining his fingers inching downward across the slippery silk of her sex-flesh, finding the core of her, he closed his eyes and swallowed, hard.

'We're there,' he announced, hoarsely, as the car drew to a halt outside the house.

'Later, then,' Alex murmured in his ear as he took his hand from her lap.

Jason didn't say anything, though the look he

shot her spoke volumes. *Later* would suit Jason Duval just fine, but for now he didn't want the complication of being caught with his cock in her hand by a friend. Reluctantly, she pulled back, just as Matt turned round, alerted by the cessation of movement.

Jason lived in a four-storeyed terraced house bordering one of the capital's finest parks. Set behind forbidding, spike-topped iron railings, the walls were thick and solid, insulating the neighbouring properties from noise and nuisance.

It was a good thing they did, Matt thought as they stepped through the door, for the fine Victorian floor tiles seemed to vibrate with the beat of the music. Jason had gutted the house, turning the entire first floor into one huge living-room. They headed there now, bursting into the room which was already almost full.

'Looks like the party's started without you,' Matt remarked, looking around him.

Jason grinned, unfazed by what appeared to be an invasion of his property.

'Parties never really start till I arrive,' he shot back before disappearing into the throng.

Matt glanced at Alex, who was clinging to his arm.

'Happy now?' he said, noticing the brightness of her eyes as she scanned the room.

She was about to answer when Steve Grainger joined them.

'So this is where it's at, is it?' he said, looking directly at Alex and effectively ignoring Matt.

Matt felt himself bristling with dislike. There was something about Steve Grainger that put his back up, nothing he could put his finger on, just a certain arrogance which grated on Matt.

Plus, of course, there was the way he treated Pippa. Any opportunity that arose to criticise or undermine her confidence, Grainger could be relied upon to jump on it. Sometimes he almost reduced her to tears, yet he was never so blatant about it that Matt could intervene without drawing attention to Pippa in a way that he sensed she would hate.

'Did you follow Jason's car here?' he asked, aware that the other man had not been invited to the private party.

Steve glanced briefly at him, but did not answer. Matt sensed the atmosphere between the other man and Alex and tried to summon up the slightest vestige of outrage that they were being so blatant about their attraction for each other. Grainger had worked his way through half the cast already, causing problems left, right and centre as he distracted attention from the real work to be done.

Then he realised that, if anything, he felt relief that Alex appeared to be switching her attention away from him. Without a word, he moved away, going in search of the wellstocked cabinet which served as a bar.

Jason found him there half an hour later.

'You're hitting that a bit heavy, mate,' he said, nodding towards the whisky bottle by Matt's side.

Matt smiled bleakly. 'Don't mind me.'

Jason sat down beside him. 'Your bird – Alex . . . would you mind much if I . . . you know . . .?'

Matt stared at Jason through an alcoholic fog. What the hell was he talking about? Then the penny dropped and he laughed.

'Be my guest,' he said, not caring a bit. 'I don't think that Alex and I will be seeing much more of each other.'

He meant it, he realised at once. After all, what was the point? They had little enough in common and, though once he would have been content to have fun with her, even sleep with her without any emotional engagement, since he'd met Pippa he knew that wasn't enough. It would never be enough again.

Jason shook his head as if he thought Matt was a lost case. Let me introduce you to a couple of birds I know – guaranteed to cure what ails you.'

Matt looked at him. His head throbbed with the effects of the music and the whisky he had drunk and there was a dull, unfamiliar ache in his groin which he assumed must be caused by sexual frustration. In a sudden, mercurial mood swing, he thought, damn Pippa and the way she had got under his skin!

'I don't know, Jason—'

'It's not healthy for a guy to come to a party like this and not get his rocks off!'

Matt laughed. He felt so confused, so ill-equipped to argue with his friend. His head ached and he was tired of trying to analyse his every thought.

'Hell, why not?' he said wearily.

Tomorrow, in the sober light of the morning he would sort out his feelings for Pippa once and for all. Tonight, he would allow himself to go along with whatever happened.

'Good on you, mate,' Jason said, leaping up and thumping him on the shoulder. 'We'll soon have you back to normal!'

Normal! Matt thought as he watched Jason weave his way through the heaving throng. What the hell was that? Aware that he had drunk a little too much for cohesive thought to flourish, Matt gave up trying to think and told himself to simply go with the flow. Consequently, when Jason returned with a statuesque blonde in tow, Matt remained passive as she wriggled her way onto his lap.

'Hello,' she said in a husky whisper, her plump, pink-painted lips mere inches from his own. 'I'm Danielle.'

He smiled vacantly at her. Vaguely he was aware of Jason slipping away. The heavy, insistent beat of the music had gradually worked its way into his system, so that eventually it felt as though it oozed through his veins with his blood, a part of him. Danielle's fleshy buttocks tantalised the long-denied shaft of his penis and he felt it engorge, nestling in the warm cleft of her bottom, easily felt through the thin material of her dress.

Feeling it rise, Danielle giggled and writhed on his lap, lodging it more securely along her crease. Putting his hands either side of her waist, Matt twisted her upper body so that she was partially facing him.

Capturing her face between his hands, he pushed the tip of his tongue between the plump cushions of her lips, running it swiftly between them before dipping his head downward. He buried his face in the warm furrow of her pneumatic breasts, breathing in her perfume.

Danielle removed him gently but firmly, but only long enough for her to stand up and turn round properly. Straddling his thighs, she sat back down on his lap, so that her crotch was pressed tight against his belly. Placing her hands on either side of his head, she pulled him back down so that he was enclosed once more in the warm, feminine contours of her chest. Pressing her upper arms against the sides of her breasts, Danielle squashed the fleshy mounds against his face so that he thought that he might suffocate.

Time seemed to slip out of sync, his surroundings shifting out of focus as he came up for air and looked about him. Jason's vast living-room was indistinguishable from a nightclub now, filled to bursting with sweating, dancing bodies. The music seemed to be building to a crescendo while the main lights had gradually become dimmer, replaced by spotlights in red and blue which raked the room in random sequence.

Matt felt disorientated and decidedly drunk. He felt as if he had been taken over by the blonde, as if she was enclosing him with her fleshy thighs and even fleshier breasts, her soft arms trapping him against her and her hot breath sighing across his cheek.

The room was filled with noise and laughter, interspersed by other, more intimate sounds, the source of which Matt could only guess at. Danielle tangled her long, insistent fingers in his hair and, pulling his head up, she held it still as she began to kiss him. She tasted of gin and lipstick and stale tobacco. It was a totally impersonal taste and Matt submitted himself to her kiss, neither enjoying nor disliking the experience. He felt like a rag doll, expressionless and limp, apart from the few inches of vibrant flesh which reared up from his groin, chafing impatiently at the restriction of his trousers.

Danielle had plans for that. As Matt watched the dancers gyrating in the centre of the room, she slid off his lap and knelt at his feet. He caught his breath as she released his cock, closing his eyes as he felt her large, cushiony lips enclose him.

His head fell back on his shoulders and the room began to spin as all sensation seem to centre in the few potent inches at his groin. Danielle was an expert, drawing the most exquisite sensations from him, making him forget everything in the moment.

Matt could feel the ejaculate gathering in the base of his cock as she rimmed the sensitive ridge of flesh at the base of his glans, her tongue darting along the tiny slit, making it weep with pleasure. The sound of his own blood roared in his ears, drowning out the sounds of the party as she drew him fully into her mouth again, her teeth scoring gently across the soft skin of his shaft.

Danielle eased her fingers underneath him, searching for the hidden, magic spot which, when touched, would precipitate his orgasm. He groaned as she found it, circling it with tantalising slowness with her fingerpad until Matt thought he would go crazy if she didn't increase the pressure.

He was like putty in her hands, so totally did she have him under her control. There was no way he was going to be able to come until Danielle was ready to allow it.

She pulled back now, leaving just the tip of his cock between her lips as she looked up at him. The sight of her on her knees at his feet with her mouth full of his sex made Matt shudder. Noticing, Danielle's eyes smiled as slowly, wickedly, she pressed harder on the small, pleasure-giving spot behind his scrotum. At the same time, she drew his entire length back into her mouth, inch by inch, so that he felt as if she was swallowing him, actually taking him into her throat.

He gasped as he came, feeling Danielle's lips moving up and down the shaft of his cock, milking him as his semen jetted out of him in a series of seemingly never-ending spurts. Danielle sucked and licked at him long after the final spasm had ebbed away, until it became almost painful.

'Enough!' he croaked, feeling thoroughly drained.

The room was spinning around him, the noise of

the party swelling and fading with peculiar rhythm. He closed his eyes, but the spinning sensation did not diminish. Matt felt Danielle refasten his trousers and rise to her feet next to him.

'Pleasant dreams, lover,' she murmured in his ear.

Gently she guided him forward so that he could rest his head and arms on the table in front of him. Matt tried to thank her, but the words seemed to stick in his throat. After a few seconds, he gave up the battle, slipping effortlessly into blessed unconsciousness.

Alex watched from across the room as the blonde who had been with Matt sauntered away. The other woman looked like the cat who got the cream, she fumed, angry that Matt had apparently responded to someone else when he had remained totally unmoved by her.

Now he seemed to have passed out cold. Alex's lip curled in a sneer. If only Pippa could see him now, she wouldn't continue to carry a torch for him for long. Prim and proper Pippa would be appalled that he could get himself into such a state.

Still, Alex reflected, her practical nature coming to the fore, Matt's behaviour had left the way clear for her to do what the hell she wanted. Cheering up a little, she turned away from the sight of Matt slumped over the table and went in search of Steve Grainger.

She found him at the bar, chatting to an ebony-skinned beauty who appeared to speak nothing but French.

'Can I speak to you for a minute, Steve?' Alex asked politely.

Steve made his apologies to the other girl and followed Alex out to the top of the stairs, where it was quieter.

'Sorry to interrupt,' she said insincerely.

Steve rolled his eyes. 'Are you kidding? The language barrier was starting to be a real problem there. I was just trying to think of a way of getting myself out of it when you came along.'

'Glad to be of service.' Alex moved closer to him, breathing in the scent of his aftershave as she put her face close to his. 'Talking about being of service . . . I've got an itch you might be able to scratch.'

Steve's eyes darkened and he snaked one arm around her waist.

'Only too happy to oblige,' he murmured.

They kissed, hot tongues pressing against each other, hands exploring, finding their bearings. As they broke apart, Alex smiled.

'Let's find somewhere a bit more private, shall we?'

Steve took her by the hand and led her down one flight of stairs to a landing. There were several doors leading off, one of which led into an enormous bathroom. Once inside, Steve turned the old-fashioned key in the lock.

'Wow! This is bigger than my bedroom at the flat!' Alex said, wandering round the room.

The room was carpeted in pure, impractical

white, dotted here and there by pale blue mats. The walls were painted gold, the same colour as the taps and other bathroom fitments, and the sanitary wear itself was finished in a deep cobalt blue. In the corner there was a shower cubicle with a wide rail running around the outside supporting a decorative privacy curtain which, when drawn, ran around the outside of the glass enclosure.

Turning back to Steve, Alex saw that he had taken off his tie and had folded his jacket over a wicker chair. He was looking at her with an expression in his eyes which she couldn't quite fathom, but which thrilled her nonetheless.

'I'd like to see you bound, naked, against that shower cubicle,' he said.

Alexandra's eyes widened in surprise. His words had been totally unexpected, and yet she found herself responding to them in a way that she would never have imagined. Normally, she liked to be the one taking the initiative, giving the orders, and it surprised her that she should welcome a turning of the tables.

Steve was watching her steadily, waiting for her to make the next move. He was very handsome in his white shirt and black, formal trousers. His dark-blond hair was tousled and now, at three in the morning, she could see the beginning of a beard pushing through his skin. His pale blue eyes glittered in the subdued lighting of the bathroom, signalling a dark desire that found an answering call deep inside her belly.

She wouldn't have minded seeing *him* bound,

naked, against the glass cubicle. If only she had her box of tricks with her ... but she didn't, and she realised that she was quite glad. Steve clearly had plans for her. It would be interesting to find out what he had in mind.

Alex allowed a smile to spread slowly across her face. Steve moved forward, and she felt her stomach clench with sudden excitement. There was something about the way he was looking at her, something dark and dangerous in his curious half smile that set her pulse racing.

'All right,' she said, her voice no more than a whisper.

Chapter Seven

ALEXANDRA'S FINGERS TREMBLED as she began to unfasten the tiny buttons which ran down the front of her top. Steve's eyes followed her movements, narrowing as she revealed her nakedness beneath.

Once she had unbuttoned it, she did not attempt to take the blouse off. Instead, she hooked her thumbs in the elasticated band at her waist and began to roll her skirt down her legs, all the while maintaining eye contact with Steve.

Again, she was naked underneath, so that once she had kicked her skirt aside, she wore nothing but the open, almost transparent chiffon blouse and her Doc Martens.

'Take off the boots,' Steve said.

There was a note of command in his voice which both thrilled and amused her. How far would she let him take this? She'd never allowed a man to tie *her* up before, although she did it often to her partners. It wasn't as if she knew this man very well, she didn't know for certain that she could trust him, and trust was all in this kind of sexual game.

'I'll use these,' he said, pulling the shower curtain tie-backs off their hooks.

His choice made Alexandra feel better – it would be easy to get out of knots made with the flimsy, decorative fabric. Reassured that this was merely a game, mock-bondage, she raised her arms above her head and rested the backs of her hands against the shower rail.

Steve's breath was warm against her skin as he bound her wrists together, then, using the second strip of cloth, tied them both to the rail above her head. He was standing very, very close, so close that she could feel the warmth of his body reaching out to her. His eyes had darkened to two deep pools of black, their expression unreadable.

Unexpectedly, he dipped his head and sucked one of her nipples into his mouth. Without preamble, he rolled it on his tongue, making her gasp. The ultra-sensitive morsel of flesh responded at once, puckering and swelling against his tongue.

'Wanton little witch,' he said before switching his attention to her other nipple.

When he was satisfied that both were as hard and swollen as they could get, he went to fetch the wooden rack which sat across the bath. Emptying its contents into the bath itself, he brought the rack over to Alex.

'Spread your legs,' he said.

There was something about those words which made Alex feel weak. Her blood sang in her veins, buzzing in her ears as she slowly eased her feet apart.

'Wider.'

She complied, feeling more open and exposed than she'd ever felt before. When he was satisfied that her feet were far enough apart, Steve placed the bath rack between them, fitting the space between the two arms at each end around her ankles. Taking off his tie, he used it to strap one ankle to the bath rack before passing it between her legs and repeating the procedure with the other leg.

'How does that feel?' he asked, stepping back to admire his handiwork.

'All right,' Alex replied doubtfully.

With the wooden bath rack strapped between her feet like a makeshift leg-spreader, her sex-lips were forced apart, leaving nothing to the imagination. The way her arms had been pulled up, over her head, stretched the tendons in her armpits so that her breasts were thrown into sharp relief, her nut-hard nipples tilted upward in an attitude of supplication.

'You look magnificent,' Steve told her. 'Just one thing missing.'

Alex's eyes widened as he produced a long, black scarf from his trouser pocket and advanced on her with it pulled taut between his hands. Her mouth ran dry as she wavered between excitement and genuine fear.

'I don't think—'

'Ssh!' he said, wrapping the scarf tightly around

her head, blocking out the light. 'It's better this way – you'll see.'

The room suddenly seemed very, very quiet. Alexandra was conscious of the sound of her own breathing, even louder than the heavy thud of her heartbeat as she strained her ears, listening. She couldn't make out where Steve was standing, whether he had moved, was close, or across the room. Never had she felt so utterly helpless and she wasn't sure that she liked it.

'Steve . . .?' she ventured after a few minutes. 'Steve . . . where are you?'

She detected a movement to her left and turned her head so that she was facing it. Her skin prickled with awareness as she sensed him come closer.

'Relax,' he said, shocking her by his proximity. 'How does this feel?'

Alexandra gasped as she felt soft bristles run from her throat, between her breasts to her stomach.

'What *is* that?' she asked him, aware that her skin had risen up in goosebumps where the brush had touched her.

'Just a bath brush.'

He stroked the brush down the fronts of her thighs to her knees, then raked it up her shins from her ankles. At the same time, he rolled a spherical object across the springy flesh of her breasts, pressing it into the undersides until she shivered.

'Glycerine soap?' she whispered, alerted by the fruity tang that was released by the contact with her skin.

'Spot on.'

Alex sensed that he was smiling, pleased with her ready participation in his game. She smelt the strong, minty smell of toothpaste and winced as it touched her skin, circling her areolae.

'It's cold,' she protested.

'I'll warm it for you.'

With small, flicking motions, Steve smeared the toothpaste over her areolae and nipples with a toothbrush. The bristles were too hard for the action to be pleasurable, and Alex winced.

'I don't like that,' she told him firmly.

Steve went very quiet. Some sixth sense told Alex that her protest had angered him, that the situation could easily turn nasty if she didn't take control.

'Take off the blindfold now,' she said, amazed by how calm her voice sounded, 'I want to watch your face while you fuck me.'

'What makes you think I'm going to fuck you?' he asked her, his tone so light that she thought she must have imagined the earlier air of menace.

'Because I'm conceited. How can you resist me?'

Steve laughed and, to her relief, stepped forward to take off the blindfold.

'I can resist you, Alex,' he said, watching her with a peculiar expression on his face. 'What makes you think you're in any position to make demands?'

Suddenly, Alex didn't want to play any more. Her arms were aching and her thighs were beginning to cramp with the effort of being secured in such an unnatural position. She was just about to tell Steve she wanted him to untie her when someone hammered on the door.

'Who the hell's been in there all this time? Come on out – I want a slash.'

Alex wisely hid her relief at hearing a voice on the other side of the bathroom door.

'Won't be a minute,' she called, her eyes challenging Steve to untie her.

He did so, rubbing her wrists and ankles solicitously before passing her her clothes.

'We'll finish this some other time,' he told her.

Alex looked at him and realised that it wasn't a game to Steve.

'Yes,' she told him carefully, instinctively knowing that it wouldn't be wise to anger him, 'let's.'

He caught hold of her arm, his fingers pinching painfully hard into her flesh. His eyes were overly bright, the pupils dilated with excitement.

'We could have fun, you and me,' he said with an intensity that made her feel uneasy.

Alex stared at him, aware that this looked very unlike the man who was welcomed into a million living-rooms every Saturday night because of his genial, easy-going humour. The man who was gazing at her so intently was an unknown quantity.

'Yes,' she replied, her unease growing by the minute.

They both looked round as the hammering on the door began again, Steve with irritation, Alex with relief.

'We – we'd better go now,' she said.

To her relief, Steve let go of her arm. Before he could change his mind, Alex went over to the bathroom door. Pulling it open, she pushed past the disgruntled party guest waiting impatiently outside, wanting only to put as much distance between her and Steve as she possibly could.

'Matt, you've got to help us out on this one.'

Lee Broadbent looked as though someone had just died. His skin had turned an unhealthy-looking mottled purple and he was chain-smoking as Matt walked into the theatre.

'What's happened?' he asked, frowning. He'd woken up with a massive hangover and hadn't appreciated being fetched by car to the theatre fully three hours before he was due in.

'It's Diana-fucking-George – *she's* what's happened! She's pulled out of the production.'

'What? But we open in three weeks . . . why?'

'I wish I knew!' Lee said, throwing down his cigarette and grinding it out with his heel. 'Her agent phoned first thing to tell me. I don't think he knows the reason any more than we do, though the smarmy bastard would die rather than admit that to me.'

'I know Diana can be a pain in the butt, but it's not like her to be this unprofessional.'

'Who cares? All I know is, we've been shat on from a high place. What are we going to do, Matt? How can we open without a leading lady?'

Matt regarded the director with distaste. Now that he needed Matt, suddenly the two of them were a 'we'. He didn't give two hoots about Diana, nor even the show, if the truth be known. All Lee Broadbent cared about was his own precious reputation.

'I'll go and see Diana, try to find out what's behind all this,' Matt offered.

'Would you? Try to persuade her to come back. It's no use talking to her fucking agent. Go straight to the horse's mouth.'

Matt sighed. His head ached and he didn't relish his role as go-between between Lee Broadbent and Diana George, but what else could he do? Without a leading lady the show was doomed.

'I'll go now then.'

'Come straight back here afterwards – preferably dragging that temperamental cow by the hair!' Lee called after him.

As Matt passed by the auditorium, he heard someone singing. Recognising Pippa's voice, he allowed himself to be distracted, opening the door quietly and slipping inside.

She was dressed in an old, grey-marl track-suit and her glorious red hair was scraped into a careless pony-tail at the back of her head. Taking centre stage, under a single, fixed spotlight, she was practising the bluesy ballad that had captivated him the first time he saw her. Entranced, Matt sat down at the back of the auditorium, confident that his presence would be concealed in the gloom.

Despite her scruffy appearance, Pippa was every inch a star. Her sweet face was transformed into loveliness as she sang and Matt felt himself melt, just as he had that first time. When she finished her number, she walked over to the pianist who was practising with her and said something to him that Matt couldn't hear.

He waited as she took up her position again, expecting her to launch into the second 'Molly Brown' number. Instead, to his surprise, she began to sing one of Diana's songs, one of the flag-wavers for the show.

She was word perfect and, unaware that she had an audience, totally uninhibited. Pippa could take Diana's role, if needed. The thought startled him and he sat forward in his seat. He was allowing his groin to rule his head, he told himself sternly. She might be good, she might be better than merely good, but Pippa Brooks didn't have the experience to carry a top show like *Chrysalis*.

She'd be a star in her own right one day, though, Matt was sure of it. Meanwhile, he was supposed to be persuading the star of this show to return to her role. Quietly, with Pippa's pure, clear voice ringing in his ears, he dragged himself away.

Though he had known Diana on and off for years, their relationship had never been intimate enough for Matt to have visited her at her home. Their short-lived affair had taken place in the location hotel and hadn't survived the return to England, largely due to Matt's indifference.

He thought of this now as he rode the lift to Diana's apartment, and felt ashamed at how he had treated her. Though he had been very young at the time, that didn't seem to him now to be an adequate excuse for his callous treatment of Diana once he stopped feeling flattered by her attention.

What must she had thought of him, of his shallow affection and cruel disregard for her feelings once he considered their affair to be over? It wasn't as if he had even been particularly polite to her during rehearsals for *Chrysalis*, fearing, he realised now, that she might misinterpret friendliness as a desire on his part to rekindle their affair.

There was no reply when he knocked on her door. Something, though, some instinct that compelled him to stay, told him that there was someone at home. He knocked again, pushing up the letterbox this time so that he could see into her hallway. There was no sign of life, but the door off the hallway was ajar, allowing a sliver of electric light to spill out onto the carpet. Why was the light on at this time in the morning? Matt frowned, sensing that all was not as it should be.

'Diana?' he called through her letterbox. 'Diana, it's me – Matt. I know you're in there, Diana, please come to the door.'

Still there was no response. Matt straightened, wondering how best to proceed. For some reason, he thought of Pippa. Recalling how she had reacted when he arrived, unannounced on her doorstep, he wondered if Diana might react in the same way.

Something was wrong, he was sure of it. Perhaps if he brought Pippa back with him, Diana would open the door and they could get to the bottom of the problem.

Feeling better now that something was decided, Matt headed back to the Connaught.

Pippa felt so happy, dancing and singing to the empty auditorium. Peter, her pianist, had been happy to meet her in the mornings when the theatre was all but empty so that she could practise whatever she chose. He applauded her now as she finished Diana George's big number, and she gave him a little curtsey.

'That was fantastic! Your voice was made for the lead role, Pippa,' he told her.

If Peter hadn't been happily ensconced with his boyfriend of the past three years, Pippa would have thought he was giving her a line. As it was, she flushed with delight at his praise, knowing that he was not the sort of person who would offer it undeservedly.

'Thank you, Peter,' she said, kissing him lightly on the cheek. 'The quality of the pianist helps, of course.'

'Naturally. Seriously, though, Pippa – something happens to you when you step under the spotlight. It's as if the limelight switches you on.'

Pippa wiped her face and neck with a towel and gazed wistfully at the now darkened stage.

'I feel like a different person out there. It's not the audience – at least, I don't think it is. It's the *freedom* of being someone else.' Feeling Peter's eyes resting thoughtfully on her, Pippa glanced at him and gave him a rueful smile. 'Pretty crazy, eh?'

He smiled at her.

'I wouldn't say that, Pippa,' he said gently. 'But I do think it's a little bit sad.'

'Sad?' Pippa repeated, surprised.

'That you feel that way. A lovely girl like you shouldn't have to live her life through the characters she plays.'

Pippa felt sudden tears prick her eyelids. Embarrassed, she pretended to be relacing her trainer.

'Well, it takes all sorts, doesn't it?' she said lightly, discouraging any further personal remarks.

After the private practise time with Peter, Pippa decided to grab a sandwich at a nearby coffee shop before going back to the theatre for the regular rehearsal. As she headed along the pavement, someone called her name. Turning, she saw Matt hurrying to catch up with her, and swore she felt her heart miss a beat.

The unexpectedness of meeting him caught her with her guard down, unable to stop the rush of pleasure which she always felt when she saw him. It must have shown on her face, for, as Matt caught up with her, he looked taken aback, then unmistakably pleased.

'Pippa – I'm glad I caught you,' he said.

'Is there something wrong?'

Matt shrugged slightly.

'I'm not certain, but there could be.' He filled her in on the shock announcement that morning of

Diana's resignation from the show.

'That's awful!' Pippa said. 'Do you know why?'

'Lee sent me round to her flat to find out. The thing is, she's not answering her door. That's why I thought of you.'

'I'm sorry? What can I do?'

Matt looked sheepish. 'Well, I was thinking that, if I had a woman with me, maybe Diana might be more inclined to let me in.'

Pippa raised her eyebrows. 'Are you such a threat, to her, Matt?'

'Of course not! But . . . you probably read about Diana and me. We had a . . . well . . .'

'An affair?' Pippa supplied helpfully.

'Yes. It was a while ago, but it didn't end too well.'

'You seem to have overcome your differences well enough to be able to work together,' Pippa commented reasonably.

'Yes. But going into her flat . . . that's different, isn't it? I was going to contact the manager, you see, ask if there's a pass-key.'

Pippa regarded him shrewdly. 'I get the feeling that you want me to come with you to make *you* feel more comfortable rather than Diana. Are you afraid she's going to jump on you?'

'Don't be ridiculous!' Matt's frown was uncharacteristically fierce. 'Look, are you going to come with me or aren't you?'

Realising she had touched a raw nerve, Pippa laughed.

'All right,' she agreed, 'I'll come. But you'll have

to buy me lunch afterwards or I'll never make it through rehearsal.'

Matt grinned, his agitation slipping away. 'It's a deal,' he said, relieved that she had agreed to help.

Back at Diana's flat, Pippa watched as Matt hammered on the actress's door.

'Open up, Diana,' he called through the letterbox. 'I've got Pippa Brooks with me – won't you at least talk to her?'

Exasperated, he turned to Pippa.

'You have a look,' he suggested.

Feeling rather foolish, Pippa bent down and looked through the letterbox. Matt was right; the living-room light did appear to be on. A curious cat watched her from the hallway whilst another stalked hopefully around an empty food bowl.

'She's not fed her cats,' she said, beginning to feel concerned herself now. 'There are several empty bowls in the hallway. What a curious place to feed them.'

'Diana has a phobia about kitchens. If she fed the cats in there she'd probably feel faint!'

He knows her far better than he'd like people to think, Pippa thought to herself. She couldn't decide, for the moment, whether the fact that he retained such information about someone with whom, by his own admission, he had had a casual affair made him less or more of an insensitive boor. He seemed genuinely concerned about Diana now, though, and she was glad to be able to decide to give him the benefit of the doubt. Opening the letter flap again, she called, 'Diana? It's Pippa – Molly Brown. I'm sorry to barge in on you, but everyone's worried ... could you at least let us know that you're all right?'

'What *do* you think you're doing?'

Pippa straightened to find a straight-backed lady of advancing years staring suspiciously at them from her own doorway. Her hair was the shade of silver that could only come out of a tube and she wore silver-rimmed spectacles which looked as if they dated from the 1950s. Pippa saw the realisation dawn in her magnified eyes as she recognised Matt, and her greying complexion flushed with pleasure.

'It is you, isn't it?' she said.

Accustomed to such nonsensical questions, Matt switched on the smile he reserved for lady fans of a certain age and advanced, his hand outstretched.

'It is indeed,' he said, capturing her right hand between both of his, 'but you have the advantage of me, Mrs...?'

'Amelia Stevenson-Jones – Miss,' she replied, flushing girlishly. 'My, oh my, first Steve Grainger, now Matt Jordan! Miss George certainly has celebrities beating a path to her door these days! Not that she isn't a celebrity herself, of course,' Miss Stevenson-Jones added hastily. 'Diana George is a legend!'

'Indeed she is,' Matt agreed, frowning as he saw how Pippa had paled at the mention of her stage husband. Realising that this was the most pertinent part of the woman's speech, he turned back to her. 'Did you say Steve Grainger's been here?'

'Yes – last night.' She leaned forward conspiratorially and dropped her voice to a loud whisper. 'For all I know, he's still in there – you know what these theatrical types are like – they don't have the same moral code as the rest of us. Oh!' Her hand flew to her mouth as she realised what she had said and to whom. 'No offence meant, Mr Jordan!'

'None taken,' he assured her, 'and please – call me Matt.'

He waited while Miss Stevenson-Jones finished simpering before asking her: 'Does that mean that you haven't seen Miss George today?'

'No, I haven't.'

'Did she mention that she might be going away at all?'

'Oh no – she's working very hard at the moment, on a new musical, so I understand. Isn't she answering her door? She's in there, you know – I'd have heard if she'd gone out because I've been in myself since yesterday lunchtime. The front door creaks, you see. I've told the maintenance manager, but what can you do?' She shrugged with the resignation of someone who didn't expect anyone to heed what she said, but kept on trying to be heard anyway.

'It must be that she hasn't heard me knocking,' Matt said now. 'If you'll excuse me . . .'

'You don't think she's ill, do you? Here – let me fetch the spare key. Miss George leaves it with me so that I can feed her cats while she's away.'

She darted back inside her own flat before Matt could say anything, leaving him waiting with Pippa in the corridor, feeling awkward. He didn't like the idea of letting himself into Diana's flat without the sanction at least of her landlord, and he had a feeling that he'd like it even less if the elderly lady insisted on accompanying him. Struck by this thought, he went and hammered on Diana's door again.

'Diana? We know you're in there! Come on now – at least speak to us. Please.' He waited and listened. Nothing. 'Diana, if you don't come to the door I'm going to let myself in with your neighbour's key. Do you hear me?'

'Here it is – I knew I'd still got it somewhere. Er ... shall I come in with you?' Her eyes flickered uncertainly from Matt to Pippa and back again, as if she couldn't quite make up her mind whether they were trustworthy.

'Would you be terribly offended if I said no, Amelia?' Matt said, turning on the charm. 'Diana is very sensitive about her image – if she's ill, she wouldn't want you to see her without her make-up. I'm an old friend,' he added, reading the elderly lady's mind.

'Well, I'm not sure . . .'

'Thank you, Amelia,' Matt said, taking the key out of her hand, 'you're a good neighbour. I'll call you if help is needed.'

Faced with Matt's determination, Amelia Stevenson-Jones returned reluctantly to her own flat, leaving him with Pippa to go into Diana's.

*

As soon as they gingerly entered Diana's living-room, Pippa's instincts told her that the flat was not empty. Apart from the cats who brushed against their legs and mewled plaintively at them, she had a definite sense of not being alone. The hairs on the back of her neck stood on end as they paused in the middle of the room, listening intently.

'Diana?' Matt's voice emerged as a whisper, and he tutted impatiently at himself, rolling his eyes at Pippa. 'Diana – are you there?' he said more loudly.

There was a sound from one of the rooms leading off the living-room, and he went towards it.

'Are you in there, Diana?'

'Piss off!'

Matt nearly jumped out of his skin as he heard her voice, though the shock was quickly followed by profound relief. He was beginning to wonder what he might be about to find. Going over to the door, he spoke to her through it.

'It's Matt. Lee sent me over to see what's wrong. I've got Pippa with me – can we come in?'

'No!'

She sounded so alarmed at the prospect that Matt snatched his hand away from the doorknob.

'Are you all right?'

'I'm fine. I'll skin the old biddy who let you in here – now piss off, Matt, leave me alone.'

'She *sounds* all right,' Matt said to Pippa.

'I don't know.' To Pippa, Diana's voice sounded

oddly distorted, as if she was having difficulty forming the words. 'She sounds a bit strange.'

'Maybe she's drunk?'

Pippa shook her head.

'I don't think so. I'm going in. Diana? It's Pippa Brooks here – I'm going to come in now.'

Diana didn't answer. Frowning, Pippa glanced towards Matt before opening the door.

At first she couldn't see much in the gloom of the bedroom. The thick curtains at the window were drawn tightly, all but blocking out the sunlight. As her eyes adjusted, she could see that the room was dominated by the bed. Advancing, Pippa saw a movement in it.

'Miss George? Diana? Are you all right?'

Catching the note of alarm in Pippa's voice, Matt strode over to the window and snapped open the curtains. Diana groaned as the bright sunlight flooded the room, exposing her.

'Oh! Go away! Don't look at me!' She hid her face in the pillows.

Exchanging a glance with Matt, Pippa sat down on the edge of the bed.

'I'm sorry to intrude like this, but Matt thought that your decision to pull out of the show was so unlike you. Then when you didn't come to the door . . . well, I'm sure you can see why we felt we ought to come in.'

Diana didn't look up, though her shoulders shook slightly, as if she were crying. Matt laid his hand tentatively on the back of her head.

'This isn't like you, Diana. Won't you at least tell

us what's wrong?'

Slowly Diana sat up, and turned to face them. As they saw her face, Matt swore under his breath, and Pippa's hand flew to her mouth. One side of the other woman's face was mottled with purple and black bruises, her cheekbone swollen and puffy so that her left eye was almost closed.

'Satisfied now?' she asked.

A tear squeezed through her narrowed eye and rolled, unheeded, down her damaged cheek.

'Who did this to you?' Matt whispered.

Glancing at him, Pippa could see he was shocked to the core. For her own part, after the initial shock, she felt remarkably calm, almost detached. When Diana turned her face away, refusing to answer him, Pippa said quietly, 'Was it Steve Grainger?'

The way Diana looked round in surprise gave her away, and Pippa knew that she was right. She felt a trembling begin inside as old fears surged to the surface. Compared to her, Diana had come off lightly, but even so, it was obvious that the actress was traumatised. Pippa felt Matt's eyes resting on her, and steeled herself for the obvious question. In the event, it was Diana who asked it.

'What makes you say that?' she said.

Pippa covered the thin, pale hand that lay on top of the covers.

'I know,' she said, her eyes signalling her empathy with the emotions with which Diana was battling.

'He did it to you?' she asked, her voice small

and full of tears still left to be shed.

Pippa nodded. 'It was a long time ago.'

'I'll kill him! I'll—'

'Go and make us all a cup of tea, please Matt,' Pippa interrupted him.

His typically masculine response was understandable, but not very helpful at that moment. What Diana needed was sympathy and understanding, to talk, or not, as she wanted. She was the most important person now; retribution could wait.

Pippa tried to convey all of this in the look she gave Matt. To her relief, he appeared to have understood, for he turned and left the bedroom without another word. Diana waited until he had gone before clutching at Pippa's hand.

'I feel so foolish!' she said urgently.

Pippa understood what she was trying to say, but did not attempt to comment, knowing it was important that Diana should have this opportunity to talk. And she did. Her words came in waves, sometimes staccato, other times tripping over each other in her haste to get them out.

Matt brought in a pot of tea, unnoticed. Realising what Pippa was doing, he stood in the background and listened. He had to keep a tight rein on his emotions, for as Diana described what had happened the night before he was unable to stop himself from imagining the same things happening to Pippa. It made everything that he had thought was senseless before make sense.

When, at last, Diana ran out of words, she wept.

Matt waited until she had calmed a little before stepping forward.

'You have to report this, Diana,' he said quietly.

Predictably, she shook her head. 'Who would believe me?' she reasoned.

'Did you make a complaint about him to the police, Pippa?'

Pippa shook her head.

'I thought the same as Diana – that they wouldn't believe me. Steve persuaded me of it.' She put her hand to her forehead in a vain attempt to stop it from throbbing. 'How many other women has he done this to? I could have had him stopped . . .'

Matt sat down on the bed next to her. When she didn't flinch away, he laid his hand over hers.

'It's not your fault, Pippa. But we have to stop him now, once and for all. Diana – if we stay here with you, will you speak to the police?'

Diana plucked nervously at the covers.

'I . . . I suppose so,' she whispered.

'Good. Pippa, you'll have to go through your story too. Afterwards, Diana, you're welcome to use my home in LA to recuperate. You have friends there, don't you?'

She smiled wanly at him.

'Yes. And my brother . . . it would be good to be near him.'

Matt looked from Diana to Pippa and marvelled at how composed they were. His heart ached for Pippa. He wished he didn't have to put her through this ordeal, but knew there was no real choice. They couldn't allow Grainger the opportunity to force himself on anyone else.

'I'll call Brad – he'll make sure none of this leaks out. All right?'

'Let's just get it over with,' Diana pleaded.

Matt nodded and left the room to make his call.

To Pippa, although the WPCs who interviewed her were kind, reliving the events of five years before was pure torture. She was grateful for Matt's silent presence, sensing his support. Having to recall every detail of memories that she had spent so much time trying to repress was more painful than she could ever have imagined.

However, she was also aware that there was a certain catharsis taking place as she talked. It was almost as if, having shored up the words for so long, being able to tell her story to other people liberated her. Like a lanced boil, the pus which had been festering inside her poured out, cleansing the poison from her system. At the end of it, she felt utterly exhausted, but undeniably relieved.

'Come on – I'll take you home,' Matt said when at last they were finished.

Diana had been interviewed and examined by the police doctor. Now she was in the bath and Brad was standing by to take her to the airport. The police weren't too happy with the idea of their chief complainant skipping the country, but Diana was adamant that she would make herself available to them by fax and phone and would return the moment she was asked. Knowing she had both the resources and the will to do just that, they reluctantly gave their consent to her plans.

Her commitment to making Steve face up to what he had done to her had apparently grown stronger as the day wore on, and her courage earned her the respect of all who listened to her. In the hours she had spent in Diana's flat, Pippa had grown to like the star. It was odd, for she had never thought it possible when they had worked together. Somehow, though, their common experience had stripped away the superficial differences that had kept them at arm's length, and it was with genuine feeling that they hugged goodbye and wished each other well.

Matt drove her back to her own flat. To Pippa's relief, she found that Alex wasn't in.

'Are you sure you're going to be all right on your own?' Matt asked her.

'Quite sure, now,' she said.

It was remarkable how calm she felt. Had someone told her that morning what was about to happen she would have expected to have gone completely to pieces. Instead, it felt as if a great burden had been lifted from her shoulders.

'Do you think they'll prosecute?' she asked as she made them both a cup of coffee.

'I should hope so!' Matt's expression darkened.

'He'll be ruined.'

'You feel sorry for him?'

Pippa grimaced at his incredulity. 'No. For so long I've hated and feared him, and with good cause. Steve thinks he's above the law, that he can do anything to any woman and no one will question his right. I don't think he even realises that what he does is wrong. Maybe he's suffering from some kind of disorder, something that can be treated.

'To be honest, I don't feel anything towards him any more. Not even anger. Is that odd?'

Matt regarded her for a moment as she sipped at her mug. She looked pale and tired, but calm, and he had the feeling she was going to be all right.

'I don't think so,' he said at last. 'Can we talk, tomorrow?'

Pippa's eyes met his and he caught his breath as he recognised the expression in them. Hope lifted his heart.

'I'd like that,' she said quietly.

Matt put down his cup.

'I'll leave you now, then, to get some sleep. Pippa?' he said as he reached the door.

She looked at him quizzically.

'What you described . . . what he did to you . . . I just want you to know that . . . I think you are so very brave, to have coped the way you have.'

'Is that what I've done, do you think? I wonder . . . ?'

Matt's heart contracted at the almost wistful expression in her eyes. Then she smiled and it was as if a light had been switched on.

'I think that now I'll be able to move on.'

'I hope so,' he said softly.

He longed to go over and kiss her, but knew instinctively that it was too soon, that he could lose her if he moved too fast.

'Until tomorrow, then.' He closed the door softly behind him.

Chapter Eight

ALEXANDRA STRETCHED FROM top to toe, like a cat, waking up every nerve and sinew. The man beside her in the king-sized bed stirred, then wakened. Staring at her through bleary eyes, he frowned sleepily.

'What time is it?'

Alex shrugged. 'Who cares? You're not in a rush, are you?'

Jason Duval caught his breath as her hand found his rising cock and caressed it knowingly.

'Matt must be mad, letting you slip through his fingers,' he said, his voice husky as she began to masturbate him.

'Let's not talk about Matt,' Alex murmured, nibbling gently on his ear.

'Suits me,' Jason gasped as her fingernail traced the tiny slit at the end of his penis.

After the debacle with Steve Grainger the night before, Alex had been relieved to literally bump into Jason as she fled from the bathroom.

'Hey – not leaving already, are you?' he'd said,

placing his hands on her elbows to steady her. 'What happened to the "later" you promised me in the car, then?'

Remembering the teasing promise, and catching sight of Steve entering the room, his eyes scanning the crowd for her, Alex manoeuvred herself so that she was shielded from sight by Jason's body. Keeping half an eye on Steve, she conjured up a smile.

'Is it too early for "later" to be "now"?' she asked him.

She must be a far better actress than even she had thought, Alex realised as Jason's eyes lit up. He hadn't seemed to notice her agitation, nor was he in the least bit suspicious of her haste.

'This way,' he said.

To her relief, they headed to the back of the room where a locked door led to the back stairs. Securing the door behind him, Jason turned and took her in his arms.

His kiss was tentative at first, and respectful. Whether it was relief that she had escaped what could have been a very unpleasant situation upstairs, or whether the urges which Steve had woken within her before she began to feel uneasy about him were lying dormant, Alex did not know. All she did know was that she wanted to wipe the memory out of her mind, at once. There was only one way she knew to do that.

Jason had been surprised, but more than happy to respond to the sudden thrust of her tongue in his mouth as she moulded her body against his.

His body responded immediately, hardening against her softness, adding to her mounting sense of urgency.

Together they slid down the wall onto the carpeted landing. The sounds of the party still taking place behind the locked door were muted, as if they were a long way away, rather than in the same house. Caught up in Alexandra's urgency, Jason curled his fingers under the hemline of her narrow skirt, and rolled it slowly up her legs.

The sensation of the fabric moving against her skin made Alex moan, and she moved her pelvis restlessly against his. Jason's fingers encountered the moist heat of her sex, unencumbered by underwear, and he lost control.

Unfastening his trousers, he knelt on the first step and manoeuvred her so that her legs were positioned on either side of his hips. Without further ado, he thrust into her, moaning as her hot, narrow passage enclosed him, the pleated inner flesh rippling along the length of his cock.

'Je-sus, Alex!' He gasped as she tangled her fingers in his hair and dragged his face against her breasts.

Alex closed her eyes, concentrating single-mindedly on sensation as she used Jason to erase the memory of the fear she had tasted mere moments before. It was a hard, savage and desperate coupling, but it was exactly what she wanted ... desired ... *needed*.

Jason came quickly, before she had a chance to reach the peak herself, leaving her hot and restless, desperate for more. As he pulled out of her, Jason saw the need reflected in her eyes and lost no time in taking her to his room.

She hadn't been unsatisfied when, somewhere towards dawn, she had fallen asleep, Alex reflected now as she played with him in the golden light of morning. Jason Duval was a tireless and generous lover. Forgetting Steve had been easy.

'Steady,' he said raggedly, curling his fingers over hers. 'Let me come inside you . . .'

Alex rolled over onto her stomach and climbed on top of him.

'Just lie back,' she said, meshing her fingers with his and lifting his hands up above his head, 'and let me pleasure you.'

Jason stared up at her, at her unusual green eyes, almond-shaped like a cat's, and her long, straight hair, falling now in a tangled curtain around her angular features. Her naked breasts were not overly large, but they were full and round, sitting pertly above her rib-cage, the cherry-tipped nipples pointing tantalisingly at him.

Entranced by her, he closed his eyes as she lowered herself onto his engorged penis. There was something curiously liberating about the way she held his arms captive, as if she wanted control of him, of his every response.

His eyes flew open as she used her internal muscles to squeeze the rigid shaft buried inside her. Her eyes were bright as she held his gaze, a certain knowingness in them making him feel weak. He had the curious feeling that she could see inside his head, could read his every desire, no matter how perverse.

'Alex . . .?' he whispered.

'Ssh . . . come, Jason . . . fill me with your seed . . .'

Her words drove him wild, making the blood roar in his ears as the semen gathered at the base of his cock. Watching him, gauging the exact moment when he reached the point of no return, Alex twisted her hips, grinding her pelvis against his and angling herself so that his lightly hair-roughened stomach chafed against the swollen promontory of her clitoris.

At once her eyes dulled from emerald to jade and her mouth slackened, falling open. Leaning all her weight on the hands that held his wrists above his head, she ground her clitoris against him as her vaginal muscles went into spasm.

Jason cried out, overcome by the sensation of her sex convulsing around his engorged cock. His orgasm broke over him like a tidal wave, the ejaculate bursting from him with a force that took his breath away, jetting up into her womb with long, powerful spurts.

It seemed to go on and on and on, wave after wave of glorious pleasure, until, releasing his arms, Alex collapsed across him, panting. Holding her close to his chest, feeling her sweat, her heat mix with his, Jason struggled to catch his breath. His heart was hammering in his chest, the memory of the sense of connection he had felt with her when she had pinned him down echoing now in his head.

He could feel himself softening inside her, but he didn't want to slide out of her, not yet.

'Alex,' he gasped when he was able to speak. 'Alex . . . where have you been all my life?'

'Dancing in the sodding chorus,' she responded mischievously, quick as a flash.

Jason laughed and the small movement dislodged his now flaccid penis from her body. Rolling her off him, he kissed her lightly before pulling her into his arms.

'Not for much longer, babe,' he promised.

He felt Alexandra's lips curve against his chest as she smiled.

'Mmm!' she sighed, pressing her lips against his nipple. 'My perfect man!'

Jason was about to tell her to have patience, that he would help her career if that was truly what she wanted, but the phone rang, its shrill tone cutting through their private idyll.

'Leave it,' Alex muttered drowsily.

Jason glanced at the bedside clock.

'Shit – it's two-thirty! Let me up to answer the phone.'

He listened, his languor dissipating at once as he was told the news.

'I'll be right there,' he promised grimly.

'What is it?' Alex sat up, unselfconsciously naked.

Jason's eyes roamed appreciatively over her body as he dressed. 'I have to go to the theatre. Stay here – make yourself at home. I might have some news for you when I get back.'

He leaned across to kiss her on the mouth.

'What kind of news?'

'Diana George has pulled out of the show.' He chuckled as he saw the calculating expression creep into her eyes. 'Who knows – you might get that break you're angling for sooner than you think.'

He left her with that thought, switching his mind to business as soon as he left the flat.

'In the absence of a leading lady, we'll have to suspend rehearsals for the rest of the week, at least,' Lee Broadbent told the men hastily assembled around the table at the Connaught.

Jason Duval glanced at the two who were his fellow backers before looking towards Matt and Brad.

'What do you think, Matt? Is the show a go-er now?'

Matt took a deep breath, conscious that he had been given his chance.

'If we had to bring in a new actress to rehearse from scratch, probably not. I'd like to propose that we use the girl who was supposed to play Molly – Pippa Brooks.'

'But the girl's an unknown!' Lee spluttered, as Matt had known he would.

'She knows Diana's part backwards,' he said. Turning to the backers, he outlined the difficulties of bringing in another actress at such a late stage. 'There's no way we could open in time if we have to start again from scratch.'

'Matt is willing to work one-to-one with Pippa

Brooks to bring her up to speed,' Brad put in quietly. 'I think if a star of Matt Jordan's standing is willing to stake his reputation on an unknown, you should at least consider his proposal.'

The argument lasted less than an hour. Only Matt and Brad knew that it was likely that, at some point, Steve Grainger would also be unable to appear. Brad was certain that funding would have been withdrawn at once had any of them suspected, and that would have been the end of the show. As it was, Matt was a big enough name to sell seats on his own, so they decided to take a risk and recast Pippa as Angela to Matt's Anthony.

'That's agreed, then,' Jason said, sitting back in his chair. 'Now who's going to take over the Molly role?'

Scanning the faces round the table, he saw that no one had a ready answer. 'Matt – how about Alex?'

Matt looked at him in surprise. He hadn't realised that Alex had moved in on Jason already.

'She might be okay,' he said slowly.

'Well, it'd certainly be easier to hire another dancer than another actress. Her agent is Dolores Winter,' Lee said, checking his Roladex, 'same as Pippa Brooks. I'll get onto her this afternoon to renegotiate their contracts.'

'Surely Pippa Brooks won't command the fee Diana George could?' one of the bankers asked crustily.

Concealing his distaste with difficulty, Matt pointed out that Pippa ought to be recompensed for taking on the role at short notice.

'After all, she'll be putting in a lot of hours over the next three weeks.'

'So will you, mate – will you want proper recompense too?' Jason asked him, his eyes signalling the hidden meaning of his words to Matt.

Matt raised his eyebrows, but did not deign to reply. He didn't like to think that his own feelings for Pippa were colouring his judgement, but if they were, Jason was a fine one to talk!

After the meeting, Matt drew Brad to one side. 'Can you line someone up, secretly, ready to replace Grainger?' he asked.

'There is someone who I think could be right for the part, if I could persuade him to keep it to himself. Jed Tyler finishes shooting the current series of *Jed Tyler Live* next week.'

The comedian would be an ideal replacement for Steve Grainger, as *Jed Tyler Live* was the rival channel's answer to Grainger's show. Matt hadn't known that Brad represented him, and now he beamed at him.

'He'd be ideal. Do you think he'll be interested?'

Brad nodded. 'I think so. He auditioned for the role and was as jealous as hell when Steve landed it. I'll get in touch with him and let him look over the script. Jed's a decent guy underneath the massive ego – we can trust him to be discreet if I explain the circumstances.'

'Good. I'll leave that with you, then, Brad.'

'Where are you off to with such a spring in your step?'

Matt grinned. 'I want to tell Pippa the news before her agent gets to her!'

Brad smiled, catching Matt's optimistic mood.

'Good luck,' he said, watching him as he strode out of the theatre. Moira would be thrilled to bits when he told her.

'They want *me* to replace Diana?' Pippa gaped at Matt, sure she must have misheard him. All day, she'd waited for him to call, possessed of a desperate need to hear his voice again. After his support the day before, she felt linked to him in a way that she hoped would be reciprocated. Now he was telling her that she was to play the lead in *Chrysalis* and her head was spinning.

'But Matt – no one knows who I am . . .'

'They soon will do, darling – you're going to be a star.'

Pippa laughed out loud. 'That sounds suspiciously like a line, Mr Jordan,' she said.

Matt felt his pulse slow as he looked at her.

'Would you like it to be?' he asked her softly.

The smile slipped slowly from Pippa's face and she stepped towards him. Tentatively she reached up and touched the side of his face with the back of her hand.

Matt hardly dared to breathe. She looked very solemn and very lovely and he was afraid to do or say anything to fracture the precious moment which was lengthening between them. It was Pippa who eventually spoke.

'I wish I was different, that I could tell you that I wanted you and that would be all it would take . . .'

'But?' Matt whispered, hardly daring to believe what he thought she was trying to tell him.

'I've never . . . been close to anyone since . . . since what happened. I don't think I can.'

'How can you know if you've never tried?' he asked reasonably.

'I just know, or, at least, I thought I knew. After yesterday . . . talking about it like that, after all this time . . . I can't explain properly, but I thought . . .' Her words trailed away as she failed to find those she needed to express herself.

Taking a chance, Matt stepped forward and slipped his hands gently under her hair, lifting it away from her neck as he cupped her face. His heart leaped when she didn't flinch away as he had half expected her to.

'You thought that maybe he wouldn't have the power to shackle you mentally any longer – isn't that right, Pippa?' he said, his voice low, trembling with emotion.

'Yes,' she whispered.

She could see her own face, pale and wide-eyed, reflected in his pupils. His hands were gentle as they cradled her and she yearned to cross the microcosmic distance that separated them. Slowly she moved her head towards his, so that their lips were almost touching.

Sensing the tension in him, knowing it was for her, she brushed her lips lightly across his, testing herself. When the familiar terror failed to rise up and choke her, she did it again, more firmly this time, allowing her mouth to linger against his for several blissful seconds.

Matt sighed as, fearful of pushing her luck too far, too fast, Pippa pulled back.

'How did that feel?' he asked her.

At that moment, she loved him for understanding, for realising how much it had taken for her to make that one small gesture towards him.

'It was good,' she admitted, putting a little space between them. 'But that's not enough, is it?'

Matt winced at the note of bitterness that had crept into her voice. Taking hold of her hands, he pressed them between his.

'It's enough for now,' he said.

Pippa gazed at him, wanting to trust him, but hardly daring to. He didn't realise how his patience would be tested if he went through with this, she was sure.

'You'll be disappointed, in the end,' she told him.

Matt shook his head. 'I don't think so. Look, Pippa – we're going to be working together eighteen hours a day while we get you ready to open as Angela. You trust me to help you, to guide you and support you in a professional capacity, don't you?'

'Of course . . .'

'Then trust me in this too. I didn't understand before why you kept pushing me away. I felt sure that you felt the same way about me as I did about you, yet you were determined to keep me at arm's length. I care about you, Pippa. I think, probably, that I'm more than a little in love with you. I've never felt this way before. What I'm trying to say is, I won't rush you, or do anything that will make you feel uncomfortable. I just want us to get to know each other – in every way.'

Pippa gazed at him, overwhelmed by his little speech. More than anything, she wanted to be free once and for all of the legacy that Steve Grainger had left her, and she knew the key was in this man's hands.

'I want that too,' she told him, and was rewarded by the look in Matt's eyes.

'It'll be all right,' he told her, 'I promise.'

'I know,' she replied, realising as she did so that she was certain of it.

Smiling, she allowed herself to be pulled gently into Matt's arms. Laying her cheek against his chest, she felt the strong, steady beat of his heart against it and felt that she had, at last, come home.

'What the hell do you mean, you got me Molly? You're letting *Pippa* take on the lead?'

Jason stared at Alex, completely taken aback by her fury. He had thought she would be pleased with her promotion – he never dreamed that she expected to get Diana's role.

'Babe, I thought you'd be made up—'

'Made up?' Alex shrieked.

Jason took an involuntary step backwards as she advanced, eyes blazing.

'You think I fucked you for some minor part? You think I'm *that* desperate?' The look she flashed at him was filled with contempt.

To Jason's chagrin, his cock immediately responded to her tirade against him. Mad as she was, Alex looked magnificent, and he knew he had to have her again.

'Alex—'

'Shut up! I haven't finished with you yet!'

Jason's mouth fell open in surprise. No woman had ever spoken to him like that before and he couldn't for the moment think of how he should react.

'Now look,' he tried, but Alex interrupted him again.

'I suppose Molly Brown is a start,' she said. 'But I'm warning you, Jason Duval – it had better be a bloody big springboard or you're history.'

Suddenly, her mood seemed to change and she smiled almost playfully at him.

'I suppose I'd better reward you,' she said. 'Now, let me see . . .'

Jason felt his pulse quicken as she looked him up and down with a speculative gleam in her eye. He'd never known a woman so sexually confident, so sure of his capitulation to her that she dared to speak to him as if he were some recalcitrant schoolboy, eager to be bent to her will. Recognising that he was indeed more than willing to submit to her every whim, Jason watched her, failing to hide his rising excitement as she walked slowly round him, eyeing him up and down.

'You keep yourself pretty fit – for a man of your age,' she said after a few minutes.

Her lips drew upward in a sardonic smile as Jason bristled visibly at her words.

'I'm thirty-seven,' he told her indignantly. 'In my prime.'

'Really? I thought men were supposed to peak, sexually speaking, at nineteen? At your age you're definitely on the downward slope!'

Jason was surprised at how irritated her gentle mockery was making him.

'Now look—' he began, his words freezing on his tongue as he saw that she wasn't listening to him. Instead, she was prowling round him again, like some kind of predatory animal. The way she was looking at his body made him feel like a piece of meat displayed for her scrutiny.

'I'm not a bleedin' sex toy!' he objected at last.

Alex looked up in some surprise.

'No? Look at that.' She nodded towards his penis which strained against the stiff fabric of his jeans. 'Maybe you should listen to your prick instead of your head, darling.'

Jason's jaw tightened. She was right, he *was* aroused by her treatment of him, but his response made him feel uneasy, out of control.

'Don't speak to me like that, Alex,' he said mildly.

She didn't reply. Instead, her lips curved upward in a small, mocking smile that made his pulse race even faster. Her fingers toyed with the buttons at her neck and she began to unfasten them slowly, one by one. Jason felt his throat run dry as he saw that she wasn't wearing anything underneath her blouse. Her breasts were full and tempting, the nipples hard and shiny-tipped. Holding his eye, Alex sucked the end of one forefinger between her lips, then circled the wet finger round one reddening crest.

'Take off your clothes,' she whispered, placing her hands firmly on her hips.

Jason stared at her, aware on some deeper level of consciousness that the choices he made now, here in this room, in front of this woman, would affect his life forever. Never had he dreamed that there was anything he didn't know about himself, that there could be any aspect of his sexuality of which he was unaware, that he hadn't thoroughly explored. But the way that Alexandra was looking at him had set up a trembling in the pit of his stomach, a sensation of wild, reckless excitement which he knew he had never felt before, and which he simply couldn't ignore. A pulse twitched in his jaw as he did as she asked.

Alex watched him as he pushed his jeans down over his hips. A thread of excitement wound its way through her system too, though she was careful to keep it hidden. She liked Jason, liked his strong, firm body which he so reluctantly bent to her will as well as the complex, generous personality that she had so far only glimpsed.

'Now lie face down on the bed.'

Jason hesitated, and she raised an eyebrow at him. Knowing that he was having to battle with himself, that his innermost desires were still constrained by his hitherto unshakeable sense of who he was, she allowed him a few precious seconds of rebellion.

'Now, Jason,' she said with quiet authority.

With a small, almost inaudible sigh, Jason surrendered to the inevitable. As he lay face down across the bed covers, Alex saw the tension in every line of his body and felt a rush of sexual excitement so intense she thought she might come, there and then.

'I went shopping while you were out,' she told him conversationally as she climbed onto the bed and knelt astride him, her knees either side of his thighs. 'There was cash on your bedside table – I hope you don't mind.'

Jason twisted his head round and she pushed his face firmly into the pillows.

'No peeping!' she said gaily, reaching over to pick a large carrier bag up from the floor.

Jason could hear the crackle of the plastic bag and the rustle of tissue paper as she rummaged inside it. Though she wasn't actually sitting on him, she was aware of her weight pressing him down into the mattress. The pillows covered his mouth and nose and he manoeuvred his head to the side so that he could breathe.

'Alex—'

'Ssh!' she said, delivering a stinging slap to his buttocks.

The surprise of it made him gasp and fall silent. A dull pulse throbbed behind his temples as the tension began to have an effect on him. What the hell was she doing?

'You have to trust me, Jason. You see, I *know* what you need.'

Jason sucked in his breath as Alex slipped a black silk scarf under his head and deftly tied it round his eyes. Her fingertips caressed his eyebrows before following the line of his eye sockets, smoothing the scarf over his skin.

'Is that nice and dark?' she purred, her breath tickling warmly over his ear as she leaned over him.

'Y-yes,' he whispered.

He'd never felt so vulnerable, so unsure of himself and he wasn't sure that he liked it.

'Good boy. Don't look so worried – I'm not going to hurt you. Not tonight, anyway. I bought some oil when I was out. If you lie very still, I'll give you a relaxing massage. All right?'

A massage! Jason felt weak as the relief flooded over him. For a moment he had thought—

'And then, if you're very, very good, I'll spank you.'

'What?'

Alex laughed, a high, tinkling laugh that was curiously musical.

'Relax, darling. Trust baby to give you what you want.'

Jason had half a mind to get up, to tell her that enough was enough. What kind of a man did she think he was? But the touch of her warm fingers slipping over his shoulders as she smoothed the musky-smelling oil over his skin made him sigh with pleasure. He'd lie, acquiescent, for a massage.

If she tried the other thing ... well ...

'Is that good?' she murmured against his ear.

'Mmm!'

He smiled. There was something very relaxing about being blindfolded like this. Rather like being in a flotation tank, he felt as if the sheer isolation removed him from stress, sharpened his other senses.

'Lift your arms up, above your head.'

Without thinking, he responded to the persuasion in her tone and slid his hands up, linking them together on the pillows. He started as he felt cold metal encircle his wrists and the handcuffs clicked into place.

'Alex—'

'Quiet!'

She climbed off the bed and pulled sharply on the chain which attached the two bracelets and he heard a second clasp being closed around the bedhead.

'There,' she said, more seductively, 'don't worry – you'll get used to it. You got used to the blindfold, didn't you?'

'This is different, I—'

'Nonsense! This is just the beginning. Don't kick.'

Jason felt panic block his throat as she suddenly dragged his legs apart and, before he had time to react, fastened each ankle to opposite corners of the bed. Alexandra's hands were gentle as she massaged the oil into his legs and arms. He could feel it running in warm rivulets down his sides, dripping onto the soft coverlet.

Behind the blindfold, Jason pictured himself lying naked and oiled face down on the bed. His arms were stretched above him, his legs pulled apart, exposing the dark cleft between his buttocks and the heavy, vulnerable sac of his balls. He gasped as Alex's fingers brushed across the delicate, hair-roughened skin, and she chuckled wickedly.

'I have you just where I want you now, don't I, lover,' she said wickedly. 'Now then – what shall I do with you?'

'Heh!'

Jason cried out as Alex slapped him hard on each buttock. The sound of flesh on flesh was almost as shocking as the sharp, stinging pain that ripped through him and he tried to get up.

'Oh, sweetie . . . that didn't really hurt, now did it?' Alex crooned, stroking his burning cheeks with a gentle hand.

Jason found the warmth spreading, becoming embarrassingly pleasant as she soothed the abused flesh. To his shame, he realised that the slaps had made him harden, so that his penis pressed into the mattress, chafing at its restriction. He wanted to roll over, to grab hold of Alex and reassert his dominiance over her. He wanted to feel like a *man* again.

As if reading his thoughts, Alex kissed the sensitive spot behind his ear.

'I'm going to roll you over now, darling. If you promise to lie still for baby I'll leave the cuffs off. Okay?'

Jason nodded, not able to trust himself to speak. The relief that washed over him as Alexandra released the cuffs from his wrists and ankles was frankly indescribable. Obediently he allowed her to position him on his back, his arms above his head again, out of her way. She refused to take off the blindfold.

'Trust me,' she said again.

Jason could hear the sound of her removing her clothes and he longed to rip the scarf away from his eyes so that he could see her. Something stopped him, though, a sense that she would ensure he would derive more pleasure from doing things her way. That must mean that he did, indeed, trust her. The thought popped into his head, clear as a clarion, taking his breath away as he realised the enormity of the realisation.

He trembled as he felt the bed dip under her weight again. The soft skin on the insides of her knees pressed against his hips as she straddled him. He could smell the scent of her arousal, could feel the heat of her open sex as she lowered it against his balls.

He groaned in disappointment as he realised that she wasn't going to allow him to enter her, and Alex laughed softly.

'This is *my* game, darling. Do as I say, or I'm taking my ball home.'

She began to slide her wet, open sex along the length of his penis, back and forth, masturbating herself against his straining shaft. Jason could feel her warm, viscous juices lubricating his cock, her soft, slippery inner flesh causing a friction which could have only one result.

Alex began to gasp and sigh as she butted her clitoris rhythmically against the exposed tip of his penis. Jason imagined her, wild-haired, wild-eyed, open-mouthed as she neared her climax and he felt the ejaculate gathering at the base of his balls.

'Oh ... oh baby ...' he moaned as he felt her sensitive flesh spasm against his.

'That's right,' Alex whispered, rubbing her breasts against his face, spurring him on, 'come for baby now ...'

Jason yelled as he came, tearing off the blindfold so that he could watch his sperm spatter her naked skin. Alex fell against his chest so that they were stuck together, her mouth finding his in a kiss so deep, so intense that it prolonged the moment of orgasm to an almost painful degree.

Holding her face between his hands, Jason kissed her forehead, her nose, her chin, her cheeks, murmuring imprecations of bliss, almost incoherent with emotion.

'That was wonderful,' he gasped when at last he was capable of coherent speech. 'You're something else, Alex. You'll get your leading roles, if that's what you want. You can have anything I can give you – just name it.'

Alex laughed and kissed him. Gently pressing him back down onto the bed, she laid her head on his shoulder, content to listen to his heartbeat as he drifted off to sleep.

Anything she wanted. Gazing up at his face, Alex

wondered, for the first time in her life, whether she might not want something other than stardom. Something that she could only find with this man, who was already in thrall to her, and who wanted to give her the world.

Chapter Nine

STEVE GRAINGER DIDN'T turn up for the first rehearsal of the reconstituted cast.

'Where the hell is he?' Lee Broadbent roared.

Matt, who had been told by Brad that Grainger had been taken in by the police for questioning, caught Pippa's eye. She looked pale, but composed, and he gave her a wink.

'We can start without him,' he said calmly. 'Once you've briefed the full cast, we'll all be splitting into smaller groups anyway.'

'That's not the point!' Lee ran his hand through his thinning hair in a gesture of exasperation. 'This show is jinxed! First Diana, now Grainger . . .' He trailed off as the entire cast collectively sucked in their breath. 'Je-sus! You don't think—'

'No!' Matt said firmly, catching Pippa's horrified expression as she realised what everyone was thinking. 'There's no way that Diana and Steve are connected. I know Diana, remember? And I've already told you she's in LA. If any stupid rumours start flying out of this building the press will go crazy. Now, can we get on with this rehearsal, or what?'

Finally, some semblance of order was created and rehearsals got underway. Pippa felt sick as she followed Matt into a side room.

'Someone's bound to talk!' she said as she closed the door behind her.

Matt sighed. 'I know. The PR guys will do what they can to keep a lid on things, but let's face it, in their book, any publicity for the show is good publicity.'

'Matt! We can't let them get away with linking Diana and Steve in that way, it's . . . it's obscene! Think what it would do to Diana if she read something like that!'

Matt looked at her and realised that she wasn't coping nearly as well as she wanted him to believe. Gently he reached forward to brush her hair back from her face.

'Pippa—'

'Hi, guys – sorry I'm late!'

They both whirled round as Pete, the pianist, burst through the door. He took one look at their faces and threw up his hands.

'I didn't mean to interrupt!' he said, turning back towards the door.

'You're not interrupting anything, Pete,' Pippa said hastily. 'Please – we really must get started. There's so much for me to learn.'

'You'll be absolutely *fine*, sweetcakes. Isn't that right, Mr J?'

'Sure is. Let's take it from the top shall, we? Act

One, Scene One, the first number.'

Pippa felt the adrenalin begin to course through her veins as Pete began to play and she took up her position with Matt. The small rehearsal room was bare and echoey, yet within minutes she felt they had made it their own small world. The part of Angela was a dream, giving Pippa the chance to use the full range of her voice as never before. It was the role she had always dreamed of playing, a vehicle that could take her wherever she wanted to go – or trip her up so that she fell flat on her face and into permanent obscurity. She was determined that nothing, but nothing, was going to stop her now, not even Steve Grainger's ominous shadow over the production.

Matt had been a revelation as Antony, even those who had had reservations about the casting had been forced to eat their words. Now, singing with him, dancing with him, rehearsing the musical scene by scene, Pippa knew she couldn't have hoped for a better co-star for her first starring role.

'You're going to knock 'em dead, Pippa,' Matt told her after that first exhilarating, exhausting rehearsal.

Leaving the rehearsal room with his words ringing in her ears and his exuberant, smacking kiss on her lips, she ran into Alex on the stairs.

'Pippa! I'm glad I've seen you – we have to talk.'

Pippa eyed her flatmate warily. She was wearing shades of acid pink and purple that made Pippa's eyeballs ache. Her hair was pulled into an untidy knot on the top of her head and her eyes were were almost feverishly bright. They'd barely seen each other to speak to since Alex had begun dating Matt and Pippa wasn't sure what there was to say. Alex, however, seemed to be in a friendly mood and she agreed to go for coffee.

'Congratulations, by the way,' Alex said as they found a seat. 'I'm sure you'll do a better job of Angela than that old trout Diana ever could!'

Pippa smiled faintly.

'Diana wasn't *that* bad!' she said, finding herself feeling protective towards the former leading lady.

Alex's eyebrows rose. 'No? You know what I think? I think she ran out on the show because she knew she stank. Can you imagine the damage the bad reviews would have done to her career? It's not as if her star's been in the ascendant for a good few years anyway. Her performance in *Chrysalis* would have sent it plummeting back down to earth.'

Pippa remained silent, knowing she couldn't divulge the real reason for Diana's departure to Alex, yet wishing that she could. It didn't seem right, somehow, to listen to Alex bad-mouth Diana in the circumstances.

'How are you getting on with Molly Brown? It was the role you wanted, wasn't it?' she asked, changing the subject.

'Oh no, darling, it was *your* part I wanted. But I'm not good enough for that.'

Pippa looked at her in surprise and Alex smiled.

'I notice you don't leap to correct me! To be honest, Pip, I'm kind of . . . ah . . . re-evaluating things right now.'

'Why? Who are you sleeping with?' Pippa said flippantly.

To her surprise, Alex flushed and she dropped her eyes.

'Jason Duval,' she replied with her usual candour.

'Wow! I'm surprised you *didn't* get my part, now that you're playing with the big boys!'

'Actually, that's why I wanted to talk to you. Jason's asked me to move in with him.'

'It's serious, then?' Alex had never shown any sign of wanting to compromise her independence before and Pippa realised that this relationship must be different. Alex looked up and held her eye.

'I hope so,' she said quietly. 'Can you manage the rent on the flat on your own now that you're on a star's salary?'

Pippa laughed shortly. 'I wish! But yes, I should be able to manage. I'm . . . I'm glad you're happier, Alex.'

Alex smiled, somewhat sheepishly.

'I used to be so jealous of you, Pip.'

'*You*, jealous of *me*?' Pippa was incredulous. Alex had everything going for her while she had been so scared of her own shadow she might never have got her break if it hadn't been for Diana's misfortune, and Matt's faith in her. She smiled gently to herself, remembering his praise and realising just how much that faith meant to her.

'Yeah. You're so talented, and I don't think you even knew it. Then there's Matt.'

'I don't think I want to talk about Matt, Alex.'

Alexandra shrugged.

'I have a confession to make about him. You see, I engineered the whole thing with Matt. I'm pretty sure now that he only went out with me so that he could find out more about you. He's crazy about you, Pip. Well, he must be – the guy never laid so much as a finger on me in all the time we went out together, and believe me, that's not usual!'

Pippa looked at her open-mouthed. ' But you said—'

'That he was all over me all the time? Yeah, I know. I lied.'

'But why?'

Alex shrugged again. 'Ego, mostly. And to make you jealous. It made me feel good to have something that you wanted, even if it *was* all a sham. Anyway, now you know. Like I said, he's crazy about you, Pip. '

'Why are you telling me all this now?' Pippa asked curiously.

Alex looked awkward. 'I don't know. To make things up to you, maybe, if that's possible. You'd be mad to let him slip through your fingers a second time, girl.'

'I don't intend to,' Pippa said.

Alex grinned as she consciously reverted to her usual self-absorption. 'With me off the scene, you stand a real chance, anyhow. I'd best be off. I'll call you to let you know when I'm going to collect my stuff, okay?'

Pippa smiled at her, knowing that the past few months which had marred their friendship really meant very little in the face of Alexandra's regret.

'Okay. Good luck with Jason, Alex. I hope it works out.'

Alex looked almost shy as she replied. 'I hope so too. Anyway, this isn't goodbye, Pip. Once we open, I hope to carry on being Molly Brown for a while – until I get Jason just where I want him.'

'Then what? Wedding bells and a transformation into a lady who lunches?'

Alex made a face at the idea. 'Well, something like that!'

Pippa watched her stride out of the coffee shop, like a bright bird of paradise amongst a flock of brown-feathered sparrows and knew that, despite her protestations that she had changed, Alex would never be content with anything less than the limelight. Maybe Jason Duval would be able to provide her with the kind of attention she craved, maybe he could hold her, and make her happy.

'I can't believe it! It's like *déjà vu*! Matt, Matt, you have to find out what's going on!'

Matt regarded Lee sourly as, two days later, there was still no sign of Steve Grainger.

'Have you tried his agent?'

'Of course I have. The man's a clam, Matt, a total clam! We open in less than three weeks – what are we going to *do*?'

Matt suppressed a sigh on hearing that 'we' again. Considering the contempt the director had shown towards him at the beginning of rehearsals, when he had presumed he would want to act the prima donna, the man had certainly changed his tune.

'I'll see what I can find out,' he promised wearily. 'But I'm not chasing over London looking for him. Pippa will be here in half an hour and we've got work to do – all the more so if we've another actor going AWOL.'

As soon as he left Lee, he phoned Brad.

'Have you heard anything?' he asked him. 'No one's seen hide nor hair of Grainger over here.'

'I was going to ring you, Matt. I'm afraid Grainger has skipped bail.'

'Christ. Do you think Pippa . . .'

'I don't know, Matt. Do you think she'd agree to stay with you for the time being? The last thing she needs right now is to let her concentration slip.'

Matt agreed, though he privately doubted that Pippa would agree to stay at his hotel.

'Keep on it, Brad. Meanwhile, is Jed Tyler on standby?'

'On standby? He's learned the part already! I'll get him down to you. Don't worry, Matt – *Chrysalis* will be one hell of a show!'

Matt laughed and put down the phone. Maybe Lee had been right when he said the production was jinxed. Whatever, Matt was determined that it would be a success against all the odds, if only because it was Pippa's first big break. Thinking of Pippa made him wonder how to break the news to her that Grainger was at large again. If he went anywhere near her . . .

'My, you do look fierce – penny for them?'

His head snapped up as Pippa spotted him.

From the look on her face, he realised that his attempt at a bright smile had failed miserably, and he took hold of both her hands. Her skin felt very soft, the bones fragile beneath the flesh.

'There's something you ought to know . . .'

Pippa felt the colour drain from her face as Matt told her that Steve had disappeared.

'What happens now?' she whispered, lowering herself into a chair.

Matt's heart went out to her and he longed to gather her up in his arms, to tell her that everything would be all right. Her body language told him that any such action would be rebuffed, and he forced himself to keep his distance.

'The police will find him, don't worry,' he said with a calmness he was far from feeling. 'Meanwhile, why don't you move into my suite at the hotel?'

Pippa's eyes were like saucers as she stared up at him.

'You mean . . . do you think he'd come after me?'

'No, no of course not. But . . . I want you to concentrate on the show, Pippa, and you won't be able to do that if you're worrying about Grainger. Hey, don't look so serious! It's just a ruse on my part to have you available for rehearsal twenty-four hours a day!'

Pippa smiled weakly at his attempt to lighten her mood. She didn't want the upheaval of moving out of the flat, but now that she was living there alone . . . she wouldn't put it past Steve to try to take out his anger on her.

'All right,' she said at last. 'I'll go home and pack a case after rehearsal.'

'Let's do it now,' Matt said, picking up his car keys.

As she followed him out of the theatre, Pippa realised he was far more worried for her than he was letting on. His concern sharpened her anxiety, but it also made her feel warm, cherished in a way she had never experienced before.

Since they had started work on the new role, Matt had been as good as his word and hadn't tried anything on with her at all. Though they kissed and more on stage, outside rehearsal hours he had been careful to keep a physical distance between them even while their friendship had grown.

Somehow, the fact that Matt was withholding his physical affection had the perverse effect of making Pippa yearn for his touch. Her body ached for closer contact with his, and her nights were filled with vivid, intensely erotic dreams which always featured Matt.

Once the barrier that had isolated her from physical contact had begun to crumble, that day in Diana's flat, Pippa had been aware of it dissolving gradually, leaving her ready and willing to make up for lost time. Being so close to Matt was like torture. Pippa longed for him to take her into his arms and love her, yet she didn't know how to make the first move she knew he was waiting for.

The idea of living so closely with him excited

her. Surely when they were under the same roof, she would be able to indicate to him somehow that she was ready to make love with him?

'Penny for them?' he asked her as he loaded her cases into the boot of his car.

Pippa blushed scarlet and he laughed.

'I guess a penny is too cheap, huh?' he teased mildly, making her laugh.

'That's for me to know and you to wonder about,' she told him tartly. 'Oh, Matt – do you think this show is ever going to get off the ground?'

'We open in two weeks, sweetheart, come hell or high water.'

Pulling her into his arms, he kissed her, oblivious to passersby, letting her go only when a flashbulb went off in their faces.

'Bloody hell!' he snarled as he recognised *The News* photographer. 'Piss off, and leave us alone! Get in the car, Pippa.'

Pushing roughly past the man, Matt jumped into the car and started up the engine. He almost knocked the photographer off his feet as he accelerated away.

'We'll be plastered over the front page of that rag tomorrow.'

Pippa looked sidelong at him, noticing his set expression, his knuckles showing white on the steering wheel as he gripped it.

'Are you ashamed of me, Matt?' she asked him quietly.

Matt looked at her in surprise, slewing the car to

a halt in a layby as he saw her face.

'How can you think such a thing, Pippa? I only thought that maybe it would embarrass you...'

'It doesn't embarrass me, Matt. I want us to be together and I don't care who knows it. Not now.'

Matt gazed at her and felt something flip in his chest. She was trying to tell him something and he sensed that a turning point had been reached.

'Pippa...' He reached for her hand and brought it up to his mouth. Kissing the tips of her fingers, he held her eye as he sucked the tip of her forefinger between his lips.

Pippa's eyes darkened as she watched him and he realised that he wanted her at that moment more than he had ever wanted any woman before. Still afraid to put his thoughts into words, he tried to convey them with his eyes. The raucous blare of a lorry klaxon made them both jump, destroying the moment.

Laughing, they settled back into their seats and Matt restarted the engine.

'Matt?' Pippa said as they rejoined the carriageway. 'Could we rehearse at the hotel today, do you think?'

Glancing at her, he saw the brightness of her eyes and knew that his instincts about her weren't wrong. She *was* ready to take their relationship a step further.

'I don't see why not,' he answered, with as much nonchalance as he could muster. Catching her eye, he smiled at her, and the smile she shot him in return sent a dart of lust directly to his groin.

They spoke very little as he negotiated the congested inner city streets in his hired car. The doorman at the hotel greeted them with a smile and unobtrusively arranged for the car to be parked in the hotel's underground car park as he opened the glass doors ahead of them.

Pippa was oblivious to both the opulence of the foyer and the openly curious glances directed towards them. Her entire body prickled with excitement, every nerve-ending aware of the man who, having collected his keys at the desk, now took her by the elbow and steered her towards the lifts.

Her skin tingled where it was in contact with his and she suddenly found it difficult to swallow. In the privacy of the plushly carpeted lift, Matt took her into his arms and kissed her.

It was a long kiss, a yearning kiss, and Pippa opened her mouth under his, allowing the feeling to flow between them. This open expression of desire was still so new to her, it provoked a feeling of joyous wonder. Yet still she held back, afraid to take the final step for fear that, at the point at which they should become one, her body would betray her, and reject him.

Sensing her anxiety, Matt pulled back gently and smiled at her. Reining in his own desire, he stroked the side of her face gently as they came to a halt and the lift doors opened.

Pippa was grateful for his consideration of her, but she missed the warmth of his long, lean body pressed against hers. Once inside the suite, she moved into his arms again, anxious to repeat the kiss and reassure herself that she had indeed crossed a barrier. If she could enjoy this now, surely being able to actually make love was but a short leap?

'Let's make some coffee,' Matt said when at last they separated again.

Pippa could see that it was taking every ounce of his self control for him to turn away from her and she loved him for caring enough about her to not want to rush things. As he made coffee, she took the opportunity to look around her.

As the hotel was to be his home for at least eighteen months, which was the length of his initial contract to play in *Chrysalis*, Matt had spared himself no luxury. The suite consisted of two en suite bedrooms which were divided by the surprisingly spacious living-room in which Pippa now found herself. The carpet was a stylishly muted blue, patterned with a faint beige trellis design. The twin sofas which faced each other over the glass-topped coffee table were pale peach leather. On the table, a vase of fresh flowers provided a splash of colour and fragrance.

'Do you always stay here when you're in London?' she asked him curiously when he returned from the bedroom where he had left his jacket.

'Usually. Sometimes I stay with my agent, Brad, and his family, but I like to have somewhere quiet where I can wind down.'

'I'm surprised you don't have a house here.'

Matt lifted his shoulders in a shrug.

'I've a beach house in Los Angeles, but I'm hardly ever there. I seem to have lost all concept of "home" over the past decade.'

Pippa thought of her loving parents, still living in the solid, suburban semi where she had grown up, still providing her with a welcome bolt-hole when the demands of the city became too much, and she felt a stab of pity for him. It must be awful to feel so rootless.

As if sensing her thoughts, Matt moved closer to her on the sofa.

'Don't look so sorry for me – one day, when I've someone to come home to, then I'll buy a whole string of houses.'

Pippa laughed. 'I'm sure just one will do.'

Matt didn't return her smile, but the look in his eyes made everything else fly out of her mind. A strange quivering began in the pit of her stomach as he traced her upper arm lightly with his fingertips, and she felt her breasts swell and harden beneath the smooth Lycra of her top. Matt must have been aware of it, but he did not take his gaze from her face as he lowered his mouth to hers again.

He kissed her lingeringly, his tongue exploring her lips and mouth, his teeth grazing gently against the delicate inner flesh of her lower lip. His hand drifted to her waist and rested lightly on the curve of her hip, his palm polishing the bone through her close-fitting leggings as she leaned into him.

Feeling her secret flesh moistening with need, Pippa knew that there was nothing she wanted more than for him to take things further. Wanting to feel the warmth of his hand against her naked skin, she imagined him working his fingers under the constriction of her waistband, edging towards the warm, moist centre of her, then sinking into the welcoming, pulpy flesh which would open like a flower at his touch . . .

She still didn't have the confidence to make the first move, though she touched him, tentatively, on the thigh with her fingertips. His muscles felt as if they were sculpted in fine steel. They convulsed at her touch and she could feel the heat of his skin even through the thick fabric of his trousers, searing her palm.

'Pippa,' he murmured, his voice thick and husky with need, 'I want you so much . . .'

Her hand closed over the physical evidence of his words, marvelling at the proud thrust of his penis against the fly front of his trousers. It felt so warm, so strong and potent, yet not threatening at all. She ran her fingertips along its length with a sense of wonder, desire gnawing at her stomach. With a small start of shock, she realised that she would like nothing more than to slip the stiff, heated column of flesh from the constricting clothing. If she could hold it in her hand, kiss and caress it, reduce Matt to the quivering mass of nerve-endings which she had become . . .

Pippa couldn't imagine Matt ever hurting her, knew, with a surety that amazed her, that she could trust him.

'Matt—'

They both jumped as someone hammered on the door.

'Matt? Matt – are you in there?'

Catching her eye, Matt grimaced as they recognised Lee's voice.

'Do you think he'll go away if we ignore him?' he asked her softly.

Pippa stifled a giggle. 'Knowing Lee – definitely not!'

'I'm afraid you're right. We'll get rid of him quickly, okay?'

He waited until she had nodded her consent before going over to the door.

'Hello, Lee,' he said, his voice resigned. 'Do you want to come in?'

'Have you seen this?' He marched in, brandishing the evening newspaper. He didn't seem to be the least bit surprised to find Pippa there and hardly acknowledged her presence, such was his agitation.

Matt read the headlines and scanned the report.

'Steve's been taken back into custody,' he said shortly.

'You don't sound very surprised! For the love of Mike, Matt – one of our leading cast members has been remanded in custody. He's been accused of rape, of all things, so there's not much chance of him making the opening night. The papers are having a field day. It's a nightmare!'

Over Lee's bent head, Matt and Pippa

exchanged a glance. Lee couldn't care less what Steve might have done – all that concerned him was the show. If the police would allow it, he'd have no qualms at all about letting an accused rapist strut the boards every night.

'Don't panic, Lee – Jed Tyler's ready to step in at a moment's notice.'

Lee looked at Matt incredulously. 'You *knew* about all this? You knew and you didn't tell *me*?'

Matt shrugged. 'I couldn't. Look, Lee, we're opening as planned without Steve, and without Diana. Pippa and I will carry the show if needs be, though I honestly don't think you need have any worries about Jed Tyler. As for the papers, well, they can print what they like – we've got work to do.'

Lee stood up and looked fiercely from Matt to Pippa. 'You bet you've got work to do. I want you back at the theatre within the hour. Until opening night, I want you to live, breathe, eat the show. Nothing else can go wrong now, do you understand me?'

'We want *Chrysalis* to be a hit just as much as you do, Lee. You're not the only one with a reputation riding on its success.'

Lee looked at Matt in surprise, as if that fact had never occurred to him before.

'Right. The theatre, then – half an hour.'

Pippa listened as he placated Lee at the door and marvelled at Matt's patience. Personally, she could cheerfully have throttled him. The news that Steve was safely in custody again was a weight off her mind, though she supposed that she should return to the flat now as she didn't have any excuse to stay with Matt. Except ... she smiled at him as he finally saw Lee off and closed the door behind him.

'Can I still stay here?' she asked him boldly.

Matt smiled at her.

'Are you kidding? The press won't leave you alone now that the scandal has broken.'

'They won't know it was Diana and I?' she said, horrified at the thought of her own humiliation being made so public. The thought of her parents hearing of it made her feel positively faint, for she had never told them what had happened to her.

'I don't think you need to worry about that. We've got to trust PR to quash any rumours that might start flying around. Anyway, you heard Lee – he wants us back at the theatre. Do you think you can face it?'

Pippa smiled weakly at him. 'I guess we ought to concentrate on work,' she said.

Matt chuckled at the regret in her tone. 'Just until we open,' he said, pulling her to her feet. 'Besides – we were going to take things slowly, remember?' He laughed at Pippa's unconscious *moue* of disgust. Sobering, he tipped her face up by crooking his forefinger under her chin. 'I want it to be right,' he said seriously. 'This is too important to rush for both of us. I don't know how I'll be able to stand it, but I predict we'll both be too exhausted by the time Lee's set us on his new rehearsal schedule to do much more than *wish* we were together '

Pippa touched her fingertips to his cheek and smiled gently. She didn't see how they would be able to sleep in the same suite and stay in their separate rooms.

'I suppose we'd better go, then,' she said, and with one last embrace, they both turned their minds reluctantly to work.

Chapter Ten

MATT WAS RIGHT. Over the next two weeks, Lee worked them all like dervishes, determined that his reputation would not be brought crashing down by a show which, it seemed to him now, had been doomed from the start.

When they weren't in the theatre, the entire cast spent the rest of their time dodging the press. Ever since the story of Steve's arrest had broken, the tabloids had gone crazy. It hadn't taken long for an enterprising hack to link Diana's precipitate departure from the cast with Steve's arrest and, on Matt's advice, she remained in hiding at his home in America.

It also hadn't escaped the hack's notice that Pippa was, to all intents and purposes, living with Matt at the hotel. Suddenly, her story captured the public imagination. It was presented as a fairytale, a welcome bright spot in the news amidst the regular fare of doom and gloom.

As the heroine of the moment, Pippa could do no wrong. She was the struggling actress who had been plucked from obscurity to play the lead when the star pulled out of the show, who captured the heart of the leading man and whose future looked so bright and rosy.

A PR assistant was appointed especially to fend off the press and to organise carefully scripted interviews which Pippa conducted with professional aplomb, conscious of a growing sense of unease.

'It's all so exaggerated,' she confided in Matt during a rare, snatched break in rehearsals. 'According to the myth that seems to have grown up around me, I was dancing in the chorus when you spotted me and told me you were going to make me a star!'

Matt laughed. As someone who had lived his life under the unforgiving lens of the press for too long, he was far more laid back.

'Count your lucky stars it's all positive stuff,' he advised her. 'Besides, it's not exactly a lie, is it? I did notice you from day one. And you are going to be a star, Pippa, make no mistake about it.'

Pippa gazed at him, still hardly able to believe what was happening to her. Caught by a spark of mischief, she told him what else they were saying about her.

'Did you know that we're about to become engaged?' she told him mischievously. 'I read it in *The News*. We are about to become the new king and queen of "luvvie-land" where we're going to live together, happily ever after!'

'Pippa – we're ready for you.'

She shot a grin at him as she responded to the unseen voice and ran to take her mark.

Matt watched her, desire trickling slowly through his veins. As far as he was concerned, for once the tabloids had shown some perception. This was the woman with whom he wanted to spend the rest of his life, with whom, he was convinced, happiness would be within grasp. All he had to do now was convince her of that fact.

He turned away in frustration, bumping into Moira who was making her way to the auditorium.

'Matt! Are you okay?' Moira's concern made him force a smile to his lips.

'I'm fine.'

'You were looking awfully grim when you turned around just then.'

Matt laughed.

'There's no hiding anything from you, is there Moira?'

She looked at him as if she wasn't sure whether to be pleased or offended.

'So? Come on, Matt – tell your auntie Moira!'

'I was just trying to figure out how to persuade Pippa to marry me.'

Moira laughed. 'Is it so hard?'

For a moment, Matt felt bleak. 'I feel a bit like that sad guy in the film *A Star is Born*. Pippa is so caught up in all this, and rightly so. It's obvious that this role is her ticket to the big time. I'm pleased for her, Moira, I can't tell you how pleased.'

He paused, and Moira gently touched his arm.
'But?'

Matt smiled, a little sadly.

'No buts, not really. It's only that, even though Pippa's practically living with me, we barely get a minute to talk.'

'You will,' Moira said confidently. 'I've seen the way she looks at you – you come first with her, Matt, don't you realise that?'

Matt gave a small, impatient gesture.

'You don't understand – I *want* her to be a hit in this show. Besides, I'm hardly on the way out yet myself, am I? We could do some good work together, as well as follow our own careers.'

'Have you told her how you feel?'

He shrugged. 'Like I said – there's never a minute to talk.'

Moira made an impatient noise with her tongue.

'Talk,' she said contemptuously. 'Actions speak louder than words. Just love her, Matt, that's all you need to do. Just love her.'

Matt watched her as she left him to meet Brad, smiling ruefully. *Just love her*. Good advice, he knew, but he'd like to know just when he would be able to find the time!

Pippa rested her head against the cool tiles in the bathroom and gazed at her white face in the mirror. Surely there was nothing left in her stomach now?

'Are you okay?'

She jumped as Matt suddenly appeared in the

bathroom, embarrassed that he should see her like this. Taking one look at her face, he rinsed a flannel under the warm tap and wiped it gently over her face and neck.

'Come and sit down,' he said, guiding her to the closed toilet seat.

'Oh, Matt, I'm so sorry! I can't face it . . . I can't do it!'

They were due at the Connaught within the hour: curtain-up was scheduled an hour after that. Matt crouched in front of her and smoothed her hair away from her sweaty forehead.

'This is nothing more than opening-night nerves,' he told her. 'You'll be fine once you're on stage.'

'I've never had it this bad!' she protested weakly. 'I always feel sick, but I've never had to spend hours with my head down the toilet!'

Matt shook his head. 'You've never been the leading lady before—'

He jumped back as Pippa made a lunge for the sink and vomited again.

'I understand now why you insisted your parents should come tomorrow instead of tonight!' he quipped as he helped her to clean up. 'Come on – you'll feel better after a shower. Once we're actually on the way you'll be fine. I promise.'

Once again, he was right. Though Pippa felt so ill even Lee had his doubts about whether she should go ahead, once she stepped on stage and was lit by the spotlight, she felt her strength returning, adrenalin taking her through the first nerve-wracking minutes until, at last, her natural talent took over.

Thanks to the barrage of publicity, the theatre was packed to the gills. Pippa forgot everybody, becoming oblivious to the audience, the critics, the off-stage staff, everybody in fact who was not on the actual stage with her. As she played her final passionate scenes with Matt, she cried real tears, clinging to him as the curtain fell on the final clinch.

The roar of the crowd brought her back to her senses as she and Matt led the cast out for a bow, then another, and another, finally receiving the inevitable bouquet, her first as a leading lady.

'They seemed to like it!' she said as they finally left the stage.

Matt turned her in his arms, aware that here, standing in the wings, was probably the last time they would be alone for hours to come.

'You were magnificent,' he told her sincerely. The excitement at seeing his faith in her rewarded was still singing through his veins, leaving him buoyant.

The look in Pippa's eyes as she smiled at him sent a dart of lust straight to his groin. Never had he wanted anyone so badly as he did at that moment and he allowed his feelings to show in his eyes.

'You weren't so bad yourself,' she whispered, her eyes never leaving his.

Then their lips met in a kiss so charged with

barely leashed passion that it left them both reeling.

'Later,' Matt whispered, his breath moving across hers in a caress so light it made her sigh.

'Yes,' she whispered.

Then they were caught up in the melee of excited cast and press and borne off in triumph to the first-night party.

It was four o'clock in the morning when Pippa finally managed to slip away with Matt, but the general euphoria made her feel as if it were much, much earlier. They had waited for the reviews to be released, and celebrated with everyone as one glowing report after another was read out.

Pippa and Matt were singled out for special praise, and Pippa was still hugging some of the remarks to her, hardly daring to believe that the critics had actually been talking about her.

'You see?' Matt said when they finally arrived at the hotel. 'Didn't I tell you that they'd love you?'

Pippa laughed gleefully. 'And you, Matt, they loved you too.'

'*I* love you,' he said suddenly.

At once the atmosphere in the room thickened and grew still. Pippa stared at Matt and knew that those three small words meant more to her than any amount of critical hyperbole. Realising that the 'later' they had been promising themselves had at last come, she held Matt's eye. It was now or never.

They were standing barely two feet apart, not touching, yet she was aware of every breath he took, sensed that her own heart was beating in unison with his. His eyes were dark, the pupils dilated already by the passion that they had not needed to simulate during their performance mere hours before.

Pippa was aware that she was trembling, that every nerve-ending seemed to have picked up on her desire and was quivering in expectation. All the moisture seemed to have dried in her mouth, in direct correlation to the gathering of honeyed fluid in the secret, tender folds of her sex.

Matt was holding himself taut, a small pulse beating steadily in his jaw. Pippa could feel the tension emanating from his every pore and the knowledge of his barely leashed passion thrilled her in a way she had never been thrilled before.

Slowly, acting on instinct, she began to unbutton the front of her dress. Matt's adam's apple bobbed as he watched her, yet still he held back, watching, allowing her to set the pace.

Pippa's dress unbuttoned from throat to mid-calf. Once she had unfastened it to the waist, she allowed it to slip off her shoulders. She shivered as the fluid fabric brushed against her skin before landing in a silky pool around her ankles. Stepping out of it, she nudged it aside with her foot before slipping off her high-heeled sandals.

Now she faced him dressed in nothing but her lacy white bra and matching briefs. The atmosphere was thick between them, the tension like a tangible thing, hovering in the air, close enough to touch. Suddenly Pippa didn't know what to do any more. She felt exposed, vulnerable and she stared at Matt in dismay.

'Matt . . .' she whispered.

He crossed the space between them in an instant, taking her in his arms with a gentleness that stilled the sudden racing of her heart at once. Pippa laid her head against his chest and breathed in the dear, familiar scent of him.

'It's all right,' he murmured, stroking her hair. 'There's nothing to be afraid of, darling.'

Pippa looked up at him and was reassured by the gentleness which partnered the desire in his eyes.

'I know,' she said simply.

The small panic attack past, she slipped her hand beneath his jacket and his shirt, seeking the warmth of his skin.

'Take this off?' she whispered, her own fingers slipping the buttons of his shirt through the buttonholes.

Matt shrugged off his jacket and threw it carelessly across the back of one of the sofas. He helped her to tug his shirt out of the waistband of his chinos and almost tore off the final two buttons in his haste, making Pippa smile.

His skin was soft, like velvet beneath the light covering of silky body hair. Closing her eyes, Pippa pressed her lips against his collarbone, tracing the line of it with the tip of her tongue to the dip where it met its twin. His skin tasted clean, slightly salty and he shivered as she she found one smooth, flat nipple.

It rose up at her touch and she drew the tiny, rubbery protuberance between her lips, sucking gently on it as she circled the other with her forefinger.

'Oh, Pippa,' he sighed as she bent her head and pressed her lips against his breastbone. She could feel the heat of his erection straining against the front of his trousers and she pulled feverishly at his belt, longing to release it. Matt pulled away from her and, watching her face all the time for fear that the panic would return, he took off the rest of his clothes.

Pippa caught her breath as she saw his naked body for the first time. She had always found him powerfully attractive clothed, but naked his beauty overwhelmed her. His body was so masculine, with its hard planes and sharp angles, his penis rearing proudly from a perfect nest of coarse dark hair, such a wonderful foil for her own feminine softness.

He seemed to hesitate, and Pippa sensed that he was afraid to make the next move in case she felt threatened by his advance. Smiling inwardly, she realised that threatened was the last thing she was feeling. Lustful, perhaps, excited, most definitely. Allowing the smile to light up her face, she breached the space between them, curling her fingers around the proud rod of his cock and pressing it against the pliant softness of her naked belly.

Matt moaned softly, his eyes flickering to a close at the first touch of her small, cool hand against him. He wanted to crush her to him, to possess her after so many months of waiting, yet he knew he must hold back, that he needed to continue to soothe and coax her. Somehow, the necessity for restraint added an exquisite tension that he knew instinctively would enhance their coming together.

Gently, he stroked Pippa's back, setting up a rhythmic caress that made her sigh with pleasure. Her legs felt weak and she leaned against him, trusting him to absorb her weight as she kissed him. His fingers found the catch to her bra and he unfastened it, drawing the straps slowly down her shoulders until her breasts spilled into his waiting hands.

Pippa gasped, taken aback by the responsiveness of her breasts to his caress. The nipples pressed against the centre of his palms, two sensitive buttons of pleasure. As Matt rolled them against his hands, she felt little sparks of ecstasy radiating from her breasts to her womb which contracted almost painfully in response.

The soft places between her thighs had swollen and moistened, her clitoris rubbing tantalisingly against the cotton of her panties. She felt warm, as if heated honey was running through her veins as Matt scooped her up into his arms. With one arm around her shoulders, and another beneath her knees, he strode with her into his bedroom.

Without taking her eyes from his, Pippa laid her head against his chest and smiled. Her entire body tingled with awareness as he lowered her onto the bed and sank down beside her.

The curtains were drawn across the window, but the soft, pinkish light of dawn was filtering through, enveloping them in a secret world of light and shadow. At that moment it felt as though there was no one else in the world but them, and each revelled in their mutual absorption.

Matt stroked and caressed every part of her body, as if exploring her. Where his fingers touched, his lips followed, until she felt as if she was vibrating with need.

'Please, Matt,' she begged him, and her voice sounded thick and needy.

It was the signal he had been waiting for. Hooking his thumbs in the waistband of her panties, he eased them down her legs, placing a kiss against the top of her pubis as he cast them aside. Pippa gasped, unused to such intimacy, and he responded by moving further up the bed and capturing her lips between his.

As he kissed her, sweetly, deeply, his fingers stroked her mound of Venus, edging closer to the soft, slippery flesh which yearned for his touch. By the time he reached the apex of her labia, Pippa was aching for him, and there was no fear as gently parted the lips of her sex.

She knew she was hot and wet, just as she knew from the way he deepened the kiss that he was pleased at her response. His fingers were so gentle as they stroked her, yet the needles of pleasure they provoked were sharp and urgent. Pippa moved her hips restlessly and, sensing that she was ready for more, Matt circled the base of her clitoris, teasing out the tiny bundle of nerve-endings until she was gasping against his mouth.

'I love you,' he murmured, his voice low and resonant, vibrating with a sincerity she knew instinctively she could trust.

'I love you, Matt,' she whispered urgently. 'Please, please . . .'

She didn't know what it was that she was pleading for, but Matt did. Smiling gently at her, he moved his finger pad back and forth over her clitoris, drawing a response from her body that Pippa had never dreamed she could give.

She felt so hot, so restless as the tension built up in the tiny button of flesh, consuming her with its intensity. Carefully, gauging her reaction all the time for fear the ecstasy might turn in an instant to remembered terror, Matt pushed her legs apart, drawing up the warm, viscous secretions from the lip of her vagina to her clitoris.

Suddenly there was an explosion of light behind her eyelids and her hips lifted up, off the bed, forcing her body into an arc.

'Oh Matt!' she cried out, reaching blindly for him as the climax gripped her.

She'd never experienced anything like this before, and for a moment she thought she might black out with the sheer intensity of it.

Matt held her until her climax peaked, then he moved so that he was lying between her legs. She could feel the tip of his penis nudging against the stretched membranes of her vagina. In the midst of her ecstasy, she tensed, anticipating pain, but

Matt's cock slipped into her easily, as if her body had been specially designed to accommodate him.

He lay still, resting inside her, allowing her to get used the sensation of being joined with him. There was no pain, only a delicious sensation of fullness that Pippa welcomed with all her heart.

She bent her knees and wrapped her legs around his waist, pulling him closer to her with her heels against his buttocks. The walls of her vagina were still convulsing with the aftershocks of orgasm and she squeezed her muscles around him, wanting to hold onto him forever.

Matt couldn't hold out any longer. His face inches from hers, he murmured sweet endearments as he began to move inside her. Even now, he was careful not to thrust too hard, rocking his pelvis back and forth just enough to give him the stimulation he craved.

After a few minutes, Pippa knew that she didn't want him to be careful of her any more. She wanted him to take her, to possess her so thoroughly that the memory of what had happened in the past would be forever superceded by their first experience together.

'Fuck me, Matt,' she whispered urgently in his ear, 'really fuck me!'

He needed no second bidding. With a shuddering cry, he possessed her as he had been longing to do since the first moment he saw her. Four, five, six times he thrust into her, carrying her with him to new heights of sensation, so that when at last his seed flooded her body, Pippa felt a fresh climax of her own ripple through her and she searched frantically for Matt's mouth.

The kiss was long and emotional, sealing their possession of each other for all time. After a few moments, they broke apart and, still resting inside her, Matt scanned her face.

'Are you all right?' he asked her, anxious now that the urgency that had gripped him had dissipated.

Pippa knew that her smile was radiant as she reassured him.

'I'll always be all right with you,' she told him simply.

Matt smiled.

'My leading lady,' he teased.

'Always. There's so much happiness ahead of us, Matt.'

Pippa's words went straight to his heart, filling it with joy. At last he had found the missing part of him, and the emptiness that had plagued him for so long was filled.

Watching the play of emotions cross his face, Pippa looked forward to introducing him to her parents the following day, and to taking the stage with him once more. All that, though, was for later. Now she had so much to learn, so much to discover. With a small, inward sigh of contentment, Pippa squeezed his already hardening cock with her vaginal muscles, signalling her renewed desire for him. She laughed as she saw his look of surprise, capturing his mouth with hers.

The dawn chorus serenaded outside their window, signalling the onset of a new day, but Matt and Pippa were oblivious. To them the night had only just begun.

Already published

BACK IN CHARGE
Mariah Greene

A woman in control. Sexy, successful, sure of herself and of what she wants, Andrea King is an ambitious account handler in a top advertising agency. Life seems sweet, as she heads for promotion and enjoys the attentions of her virile young boyfriend.

But strange things are afoot at the agency. A shake-up is ordered, with the key job of Creative Director in the balance. Andrea has her rivals for the post, but when the chance of winning a major new account presents itself, she will go to any lengths to please her client – and herself . . .

0 7515 1276 1

THE DISCIPLINE OF PEARLS
Susan Swann

A mysterious gift, handed to her by a dark and arrogant stranger. Who was he? How did he know so much about her? How did he know her life was crying out for something different? Something . . . exciting, erotic?

The pearl pendant, and the accompanying card bearing an unknown telephone number, propel Marika into a world of uninhibited sexuality, filled with the promise of a desire she had never thought possible. The Discipline of Pearls ... an exclusive society that speaks to the very core of her sexual being, bringing with it calls to ecstasies she is powerless to ignore, unwilling to resist . . .

0 7515 1277 X

HOTEL APHRODISIA
Dorothy Starr

The luxury hotel of Bouvier Manor nestles near a spring whose mineral water is reputed to have powerful aphrodisiac qualities. Whether this is true or not, Dani Stratton, the hotel's feisty receptionist, finds concentrating on work rather tricky, particularly when the muscularly attractive Mitch is around.

And even as a mysterious consortium threatens to take over the Manor, staff and guests seem quite unable to control their insatiable thirsts . . .

0 7515 1287 7

AROUSING ANNA
Nina Sheridan

Anna had always assumed she was frigid. At least, that's what her husband Paul had always told her in between telling her to keep still during their weekly fumblings under the covers and playing the field himself during his many business trips.

But one such trip provides the chance that Anna didn't even know she was yearning for. Agreeing to put up a lecturer who is visiting the university where she works, she expects to be host to a dry, elderly academic, and certainly isn't expecting a dashing young Frenchman who immediately speaks to her innermost desires. And, much to her delight and surprise, the vibrant Dominic proves himself able and willing to apply himself to the task of arousing Anna . . .

0 7515 1222 2

THE WOMEN'S CLUB
Vanessa Davies

Sybarites is a health club with a difference. Its owner, Julia Marquis, has introduced a full range of services to guarantee complete satisfaction. For after their saunas and facials the exclusively female members can enjoy an 'intimate' massage from one of the club's expert masseurs.

And now, with the arrival of Grant Delaney, it seems the privileged clientele of the women's club will be getting even better value for their money. This talented masseur can fulfil any woman's erotic dreams.

Except Julia's . . .

0 7515 1343 1

PLAYING THE GAME
Selina Seymour

Kate has had enough. No longer is she prepared to pander to the whims of lovers who don't love her, no longer will she cater for their desires while neglecting her own.

But in reaching this decision Kate makes a startling discovery: the potency of her sexual urge, now given free rein through her willingness to play men at their own game. And it is an urge that doesn't go unnoticed – whether at her chauvinistic City firm, at the chateau of a new French client, or in performing the duties of a high-class call girl . . .

0 7515 1189 7

A SLAVE TO HIS KISS
Anastasia Dubois

When her twin sister Cassie goes missing in the South of France, Venetia Fellowes knows she must do everything in her power to find her. But in the dusty village of Valazur, where Cassie was last seen, a strange aura of complicity connects those who knew her, heightened by an atmosphere of unrestrained sexuality.

As her fears for Cassie's safety mount, Venetia turns to the one person who might be able to help: the enigmatic Esteban, a study in sexual mystery whose powerful spell demands the ultimate sacrifice . . .

0 7515 1344 X

SATURNALIA
Zara Devereux

Recently widowed, Heather Logan is concerned about her sex-life. Even when married it was plainly unsatisfactory, and now the prospects for sexual fulfilment look decidedly thin.

After consulting a worldly friend, however, Heather takes his advice and checks in to Tostavyn Grange, a private hotel-cum-therapy centre for sexual inhibition. Heather had been warned about their 'unconventional' methods, but after the preliminary session, in which she is brought to a thunderous climax – her first – she is more than willing to complete the course . . .

0 7515 1342 3

LITTLE, BROWN & CO. ORDER FORM

All X Libris titles are £4.99

Little, Brown and Company, PO Box 50,
Harlow, Essex CM17 ODZ
Tel: 01279 438150   Fax: 01279 439376

Payments can be made as follows: cheque, postal order (payable to Little, Brown and Company) or by credit cards, Visa/Access. Do not send cash or currency. UK customers and B.F.P.O. please allow £1.00 for postage and packing for the first book, plus 50p for the second book, plus 30p for each additional book up to a maximum charge of £3.00 (7 books plus). Overseas customers including Ireland, please allow £2.00 for the first book plus £1.00 for the second book, plus 50p for each additional book.

NAME (Block Letters) ....

....

ADDRESS ....

....

....

☐ I enclose a cheque/postal order made payable to Little, Brown and Company for £_____

☐ I wish to pay by Access/Visa/AMEX* Card
(* delete as appropriate)

Number ☐☐☐☐☐☐☐☐☐☐☐☐☐☐☐☐

Card Expiry Date_____ Signature_____